The Winter Spider

Doc Krinberg

Aignos Publishing
an imprint of Savant Books and Publications
Honolulu, HI, USA
2018

Published in the USA by Aignos Publishing LLC
An imprint of Savant Books and Publications LLC
2630 Kapiolani Blvd #1601
Honolulu, HI 96826
http://www.aignospublishing.com

Printed in the USA

Edited by Zachary M. Oliver
Cover Art/Photo Credits to Laura Hatcher
Cover by Daniel S. Janik

Copyright 2017 by Gary "Doc" Krinberg. All rights reserved. No part of this work may be reproduced without the prior written permission of the author.

13 digit ISBN: 978-0-9970020-8-9

All names, characters, places and incidents are fictitious or used fictitiously. Any resemblance to actual persons, living or dead, and any places or events is purely coincidental.

First Edition: March 2018
Library of Congress Control Number: 2018932446

Dedication

To Zach— My ohana and cohort who always kept the door open

Foreword

"Of all creatures that breathe and move upon the earth, nothing is bred that is weaker than man" - Homer, *The Odyssey*

Doc Krinberg

Chapter 1

The year 1978 didn't start well. Oakland had the blown fumble call and lost 20-17 to the fucking Broncos, their hopes for a Super Bowl repeat done. Now, two weeks later I was even in a darker mood sitting in Elihu Fuqua's stylish house in Pacific Heights, my head from sinus to crown a cheap icebox of finely cut skinny girl waiting to see if the Cowboys could slam a door on the upstart Broncos in what was turning into another loser Super Bowl. What didn't help was I was still suffering from the effects of the Sex Pistols concert at Winterland the night before, barely sleeping due to Sylvia's roommate and her friends in multi-colored wigs doing amyl and screeching like castrati. While that might be a normal evening in some quarters of the City, I was pretty much on my last nerve.

Fuqua had a refrigerator full of Henry Weinhard's private reserve, some bags of froopies and doodads, assorted cold cuts, rolls and cheese from the deli on Union Street that delivered. Before us, next to the potato salad, a cereal bowl of coke with shotgun snorters made of sterling silver stuck out like two snowbound periscopes. This was Fuqua's style, and his persona wouldn't allow some cheap gram bottle holder from Haight Street; the bowl spoke to the largesse of his extended ego and entitlement. The Fuqua's had lived in San Francisco since the 1880's and Elihu Sterling Fuqua III never let people forget. Anyway, his designer stepped on coke, cut with baby laxative, went smoothly with the Weinhard's. Why he ordered so much food I couldn't imagine unless he had invited many no-shows. Humming on this blow like telephone lines in a high wind we hadn't taken a bite.

    I hadn't planned on watching the Super Bowl at Eli's house but he called at the last minute said he was alone and come over as he had the house stocked with groceries and liquor. His exaggerated sniffing during the conversation spoke the unspoken so I agreed. In my head I told myself maybe the first half then I would book out of there. I could take Eli only in short bursts. There was also a motive for him asking *me* over and I was surprised the house didn't have his usual entourage of either all or part of the Disney Boys, the Weasel, Francois or my cousin Jack, but then I remembered he was in LA. Eli's soul mate, my older cousin Clovis, was living in Los Angeles and it was hard to get him out of there. For one thing his wife Meredith disliked Eli's girlfriend Mona and Clovis had a neurosis about not shitting in a familiar place; it stressed and constipated him to leave the sacred confines of his own commode.

    I could understand Meredith's avoidance of Mona; channeling Tura Satana, affecting her style of hair down to the bangs and wearing nothing but low cut black tops tucked into toreador pants and catch-me-fuck-me high heels. Mona, like Tura, was half Japanese. Her appearance was unnerving to some and downright scarifying to others. She elicited perverse comments, entreaties of marriage or requests to be whipped from others. She was always braless, stretching the material of her tops and Meredith, standing on British pomposity and the belief she was Marianne Faithfull, thought her bosomy gravity defiance very low carriage. Mona's nipples were the size of bar coasters and quite prominent in her choice of wardrobe. Eli loved what he termed her 'other worldly' qualities, which included dancing at the Condor Club when he met her.

    I'm not crazy about the Cowboys but I told an unengaged Eli earlier the enemy of my enemy…blah blah blah, to which he nodded while taking up one of the shotguns and inhaling its contents, moaning in pleasure, fell back against his couch cushions. " I really wanted to see Oakland against Dallas. The fucking Broncos are poseurs." Eli loved calling people poseurs, fops, poltroons, footpads, dancehall loungers or ne'er-doo-wells. His mother lived in a mansion in Healdsburg with Eli's 4th father, disgusted by the increase in minorities and gays in the City, she stayed there almost exclusively leaving Eli to dwell in this house and manage other properties they had scattered in Telegraph Hill and Russian Hill. I had heard the story numerous times of them bailing from the City. Eli liked imitating his latest father's disgusted rant, a nasally William F. Buckley message of white exceptionalism His mother, like Meredith, was also scared of Mona.

Eli handed over the other shotgun and then leaned back taking a long pull on his Weinhard. "So…what's new with your cousin Jack?" He asked casually. I was still tilting my head back after snorting a huge hit, and with eyes closed told him I didn't know shit about Jack, which was a lie.

"He's visiting his folks and Clovis this weekend in L.A." he said, and then cursed Craig Morton for a completed pass. "Or I would've had him over too."

"Really?" I didn't know where Eli was going with this so I just let him keep playing his cards.

"If I needed you to vouch for Jack, could you? Or would you plead the 5th for family ties? By the way, you still with that *Negro* girl?" To guys like Eli it was a matter of self-control to even say 'negro' but I had inkling now of what was going on.

"Well, Clovis is family, and haven't you asked *him*? Anyway, it's not like he's an unknown quality. Certain people have known him for years. And yea, I'm dating *Sylvia*. Maybe the four of us can double date as a cultural diversity experiment. We'll go eat in Berkeley so we're not hassled." I teased, watching him frown at the idea.

He cleared his throat after another shotgun blast, "You and Jack are close, same age, and you grew up together. So, could you vouch for him?"

"Tell me why you need me to."

"He wants to make the next run to Lima."

And that's how it started. Should've known Lytle's fumble and the refs allowing Denver to recover and keep Stabler & company from repeating spelled a bad omen for 1978. That, and disco.

Chapter 2

I had dropped 2K on the Oakland-Denver game to Calloway at work. He was a Texan who now lived in Vallejo and had taken the Broncos and the points. That had hurt, but now I needed to talk to my bookie at the Asian-American club as I took Dallas to beat the hapless Donkees and probably broke even or actually won a few bucks. Francois of course was still running the book there among all his other talents to include almost every fresh Pacific island girl illegally entering the port to end up in one of his houses in either Pacifica or Daly City. He liked suburban areas more than the City proper as he felt they drew less heat. The clients were appointments only and at the strip malls the girls worked what resembled professional offices taking clients as opposed to Ellis Street flops and walk-ups that were obvious fuckpads. Elihu and Clovis knew François from the late 50's in Hawaii, so I was a legacy that had some privileges; one was having him as my bookie and 'friend.'

Francois also did favors for the Disney Boys and on occasion did some strong arm work too. Half French and half Samoan he was full linebacker material. His flat Polynesian face made lifeless by dull grey eyes that seemed to fall asleep under the downward twist of his brows was enough to make people take pause and his laugh held absolutely no humor and breathed a stout warning. He found mirth in the pain he inflicted and the money he made from his girls, his book and various dope deals. The

Disney Boys always had some gig they were working and François' phones at various residences always held messages for employment.

I hated to look at him even though I had a soft spot, but like everything else, he was a necessary evil. And he had a payday for me after my fleecing by Calloway. Sylvia had no clue of this deviant amusement and that was a good thing. I only bet big events and didn't fall into the 'degenerate gambler' category by a long shot. If she had an idea of my life outside my Teamster's gig she would probably run. Looking back I wish she had.

Who would blame her?

Chapter 3

Years ago I had met Francois in what appeared to be an accident but was actually a set-up. It happened as I was sitting in my aunt and uncle's apartment in Hollywood paying respects after I had been discharged from the Marines and making the rounds quietly after I insisted my parents not throw a party. Clovis and Meredith were visiting his parents as well and Francois, in town collecting debts at the time was also going to kill Clovis over some underhanded dog act Clovis had perpetrated against him; a falling out over money, what else? Clovis, scared shitless after having seen him in action in Hawaii against deadbeats or rude haoles, pleaded with me to intervene. I was fresh from the Corps and having finished my second tour in Vietnam still owned a lot of rough edges, told Clovis I'd help him and who was this asshole François? Meredith was shaking and had lost all of her Marianne Faithful coolness, her bottom lip buried under her upper teeth in worry. I asked Clovis how he could be so stupid as to let this guy know his parent's address and he told me they used to package ounce lids of pot there, breaking it off kilos grown in Maui, while my uncle did his day job for the city and my aunt did retail work at May Co. on Fairfax so all day they would bundle dope for dealers they had on the string, to include Jack and I.

There was a knock at the door and Clovis was quick to jump up and I could hear some muffled discussion and then he called me. My uncle and aunt were watching the Dodgers game on KTTV and waved me off after I said 'excuse me.' When I first took in Francois I asked myself what the fuck I had gotten into! He was huge and in the heat of L.A. wore a tank top that showed his immense, knotted biceps covered in tribal bands. Clovis ushered us both to a stairway that led to an upper roof deck for sunbathing and luckily no other tenants were there. Francois pointed to me:

"Dis punk gonna protect you, Clovis?" He had a heavy pidgin laden accent.

Clovis, shaking like a dog shitting razor blades asked Francois to give him more time.

"You outta time." He said nonchalantly, now totally ignoring me. I was trying to figure out why Clovis brought us up here, as it looked too easy for this huge fucker to toss us both off the roof. My hair had started growing out but still had the infrastructure for a high and tight and this guy turns his lifeless eyes to me and again ever so nonchalantly asks, " You just outta stir? What's with dat hair?"

"Marines, not jail." It was a pretty silly conversation in light of the fact he had come to break my cousin's neck. There was a long silence broken by Clovis.

"He just got back from Nam, there for two tours." As if this would scare this golem. Then a small smile broke on Francois' face.

"Corps, huh? I went Lebanon in '58. You just get back?"

"Yea, he did he…"

"Shut da fuck up, Clovis." He turned back to me, "is it as lolo as dey say?"

I shrugged, "Depends on your definition of crazy."

"Rifle Company?"

"No, Recon." Again, there was a long silence that allowed me to look out at the horizon from my uncle's apartment rooftop. From up here, on a clear day I bet I could see Long Beach. But that day it was hot and hazy and it was like this huge vacuum bag of dust and shit.

"I didn't tink anybody in dis family had any balls, Clovis. One week. One fucking week, or I'll fuck you and dat frigid limey bitch where you both breathe." He turned to me, "Semper Fi." And he walked down the stairs off the deck.

I looked at my cousin with what he misread as a question when it was only disgust. "He only respects two kinds of people; those who've done time, and those who were in the Corps. I owe you." And that was why he had me there. The Corps. Clovis is part Okie, but he's not stupid.

And of course over the years I flogged that debt like the family mule.

Doc Krinberg

Chapter 4

I moved up north and I started school at CCSF just to spin my wheels and see if I got traction in any direction using my GI Bill and secured work at a storage garage on upper Pine Street. It was a Teamsters gig so I became unionized and found a friend and ersatz sea-daddy in Dominic Rizzi, the honcho there. He was a local North Beach boy who had served in the Corps as well and was an island hopping Raider in the Pacific. He picked up some weird jungle rot or something in his jaw and constantly moved it as if he were chewing cud all day. He was happy to help me out and had moved me up the ranks from car hop to cashier to bank runs and also bag man as I took certain things to guys who were supposedly also Teamsters but they always wore suits and stayed in Nob Hill hotels. Dominic would always talk to us boys in the garage about certain matters that had come up union-wise and we would tell him how we wished to vote and he assured us we didn't need to attend the meeting as he would tender our votes respectively but we all knew it was bullshit and he cast the votes the way *he* was told to cast them. It was a smooth job and I had learned to tune his war stories out long ago. He became so confident in me he would start leaving earlier. He owned a nice little house down the peninsula in San Bruno and he liked to avoid the traffic on Bayshore, and so I started to become management. And then there were more of the side jobs. Payback from Clovis putting me onto a few things and moving some weight for him under the auspices of vacation time. I'd quit CCSF after my first six months at the garage and so had free weekends from study.

What followed was the intro to Elihu, whom I'd actually met as a kid but barely remembered, and of course Francois who resided down the peninsula and who liked me. The fraternity of the Corps ran deep, even in career criminals. So I was putting away union wages and the money from this and that and then I was doing a lot of this and that. And unknown to me, Jack was also into the 'this and that' too, but mostly for the Disney Boys who treated him like an intern. But Jack knew how to wear a suit and put it over on people so he fronted a few bunco gigs on out of towners. I would avoid any direct work for them because honestly they creeped me out but Jack wanted to be a member. That was a flaw in his character; that need to be 'in' which couldn't be reconciled. When I first met them, they had a business proposition, and Clovis, Francois and Eli had vouched for me. Lucky me.

Chapter 5

Jack, his brother Nick and I grew up together in West Los Angeles. Their real names were Costas and Nico, but they bugged their parents, my Uncle Gus and Aunt Carmen for 'American' nicknames. We lived on the west side before the *white flight* had hit the high water mark of Robertson Blvd and we all attended Crescent Heights, Louis Pasteur and then Hamilton. We were an anomaly in this heavy Jewish area as Greeks but we sort of blended in and if one of our playmates parents inquired as to our ethnicity or faith, we would just smile like a member of the tribe, and they figured us for Greek Jews. This only made the three of us tighter as a result. We did know some Greek families in the neighborhood but they *were* Jews and most of the adults had seen the inside of the camps. That whole area had people with tattooed forearms. We would see them at the A&P on La Cienega or at Big Town on Pico shopping or working in the gardens and flowerbeds of their apartments or houses. One night after a party at a Greek home on Point View near Airdrome, my mother cried as we drove home. The woman in whose house we had just partied had been sterilized after internment in 1943. She rubbed my head until I fell asleep, or faked sleep that night. Seeing her melancholy put the freak on me.

Close knit as families, we spent almost every weekend with my cousins, not so much Clovis and his family as our fathers weren't very close being related only to my aunt as first cousins. Clovis' father wasn't

Greek and that broke the bond. He was a blonde from central California and still had dust bowl Okie all over him. My parents felt more comfortable without his company and my father would always use Clovis, a few years older than us three as an example of what to not grow into. I remember him turning to my mother one night as they dried dishes and saying in Greek, 'Who the hell names their child after a town they lived in?' My other aunt and uncle who lived north of us had a daughter, Jennifer who we hardly saw. And anyway, she was a girl.

My mother was usually the only one, along with her sister who actually attended the Greek Orthodox Church on 3rd Street. My dad's family had been in the states since the 1890's and he had given up religion after the war and didn't hold my feet to the fire, as I had gone thru Chrismation after birth, and so it went for Jack and Nick as well. We attended some of the lavish, we thought, bar mitzvahs our schoolmates invited us to. We all sort of got off wearing yarmulkes and dancing the Hora and taking a blast of Manischevitz, which wasn't too different from Greek parties with the exception we drank more, retsina and ouzo tasting way better and seemed to have more fun. Nick, way more than Jack and I, really went in for the Jewish thing and almost made my aunt faint when he told her he wanted to be a Jew, but lucky for him it was a passing phase that lasted as long as he went steady with Sharon Abrahamson. When she threw him over for some guy named Aaron Katz he decided God had truly turned his back on him. Jack and I just laughed.

I wasn't always a criminal but I suppose there were elements in me that just sort of relaxed my moral code and discovered I simply didn't have any; shoplifting, stolen bikes, cars left open that yielded different things ranging from jewelry to cash, liquor and condoms and occasionally a handgun stashed in the dashboard. We fenced stuff through a guy in high school whose kid brother we knew at Pasteur. They were Irish and like us, religious outliers. I remember the older brother saying things like 'fuck these sheenies—and anyway, we Cat'lics gotta stay together.' I had no clue what he did with all this petty swag we brought in but it was enjoyable and we dug doing it, Nick not so much; always a little more serious and oh so Protestant ethic. He was a year younger than us and working as a box boy at the A&P across from Adohr Farms. Tuesdays the families would get together because it was cheap night at Piece 'O' Pizza on 18th Street when pies were only $1.10 apiece. We would stuff ourselves and while our parents started playing canasta, cruise the outlying neighborhoods for open cars and things to boost.

Saturdays was 'Jonny Quest' and little league at Rancho. Nick, Jack and I would have sleepovers and watch "Jeepers Creepers' late Saturday nights laughing at 'The Brain that Wouldn't Die' or some Ed Wood crap they featured. Sundays was the Helms truck and cream puffs then family times; sometimes a drive to the mountains, in summers to POP or the beach. Even at the beach, we would scout who left their blankets to go swim then hit the area and boost whatever. Did people really think putting a wallet inside a sneaker was really safe?

The new stadium had been finished at Chavez Ravine and we would push our dads to take us to Dodger games. This was '62 and right before high school. I had a paper route in the afternoon to cover the tracks of my and Jack's criminal enterprises and launder my real money with my swag money and I liked surprising my dad with tickets to a game. Looking back I always wondered what I could've done differently to not end up here. The only thing that could've changed it was being killed in Viet Nam. And that didn't happen.

Doc Krinberg

Chapter 6

Eli had tried to pump me a few more times but I played dumb in regards to Jack so for the time being he let it ride. Mona had come back to the house late in the 3rd quarter so I was treated to her ass bending stretch over the couch to get around me routine as well as lean over 'look at my nipples' rodeo. I had the tee shirt already but it was a fresh break from Fuqua's inquiries and rants in regards to weakness of the AFC representation.

"We don't see you that often, Remy," she said, filling her cigarette holder. "You should stop by more often. We don't get company so much." And she threw a stink eye in Elihu's direction.

"I'm just a working stiff, Mona, I don't get around a lot." My standard line, but she was looking at me differently, like when you see someone you haven't for a long time and they appear different; older or disfigured. Or the first time you really see them.

Then I had to leave. There's just so much a man can take.

Doc Krinberg

Chapter 7

I was recovering alone that night of the Super Bowl, and having done the concert at Winterland and then Eli's, I was exhausted. I lived in a nice little garret flat on Hugo, far enough away from Irving Street so I wouldn't hear the N-Judah car like it was in my front room. I had to be downtown at the garage early and I knew Sylvia was working. She was just up the hill at the USF Med Center, focused on a degree in advanced nursing. I lay there thinking about her, the idea of her, and smiling tried to pass out in the dark.

She lived in the western addition area on O'Farrell and Steiner, and I had yet to convince her to move. Her roommate Marta worked in a wig shop on Market and was dating this Portagee guy from Brazil who didn't know anything except soccer and playing disco music way loud and cooked at all hours of the night, sometimes in one of her wigs. Sylvia had laughed when I asked her to move in, her work and school almost in walking distance.

"Really Remy? I still can't believe I'm dating you."

We had met summer before, downtown. I was crossing Union Square and boom! There she was. While most women had on their crème-de-menthe colored high-waisted pants with huge platform soles she was in jeans with flat loafers and a wife beater tee shirt with the huge Rolling Stones tongue and lips. She was the anti-disco and I was just floored at her looks. Her hair was short but relaxed and the turquoise studs in her earlobes stood out against her dark skin. She wore no make-up, and there I was in a work shirt with my name over the right pocket. She caught me looking at her and then I noticed she carried a book. Student? Tourist? The Stones tee shirt hooked me. After a few seconds of warp speed thoughts I just went for it.

"Hi," I said casually as I could. Her lips smiled and she said hi back, now amused.

"Question: Stones or just the logo?"

"Stones." Now she was wondering.

"Student or tourist?"

"Student."

"Live in the City or just attending school here?"

"Now, you should've said questions," thoroughly amused. "Native."

"Navy or Marines?"

"Navy."

I gave her a huge theatrical wince of pain,"Ohhh…you *almost* had me." I snapped my fingers, smiled and started to walk away.

To my back I heard, "Greek or Italian?"

"Greek."

"Leon's Taraval or Fillmore?"

"Fillmore."

"Niners or Raiders?"

"Raiders."

She twisted her mouth to one side as if deciding on a choice of things to do or places to go. Then walking by me ever so slowly she said, "Coffee Cantata, eight tonight." And she just walked out of the square towards Geary Avenue. I pulled my shift and Dominic continued with his ritual of patting me on the back, telling me I had the helm and then added to look out for the new guy we had just hired as he thought he might be boosting shit from cars, and then he left. I smiled remembering all the cars I had boosted shit from. At five I turned it over to Calloway, made the receipts out for the day and dropped it all in the safe.

Because I had no storage on Hugo, I kept my motorcycle stashed in a corner angle spot that couldn't accommodate a car. Dominic allowed it as a perk as I habitually walked down Taylor or Mason to the streetcar stops to go home, but tonight I would take it out and ride home, and then out to Fern Bar Central; Union Street. I didn't want to rely on MUNI that night. And anyway, who can resist a guy in a leather jacket?

That was then and now its something both of us had thought about but remaining in separate lanes and with different conclusions…and as I popped up that night, again tried letting the coke and beer drain from me, coming back down so I could attempt sleep I didn't help it by pouring a drink and lighting a cigarette.

Jack.

He wanted to mule from Lima for the Board Members; Elihu, The Disney Boys, Clovis and whoever else were pongoing up for another run and an enormous payday. It wasn't so much the money invested, as the dope was cheap, it was the windfall of retail back in the States. And that also meant the Weasel would again be along riding shotgun; the invisible partner who set up the buy and helped conceal it. Then he became the shadow who followed the mule and made sure things went smoothly from there. He divided half of his time between the City and Lima with an import company sending cheap tropical clothing goods back to a small store in Berkeley operated by one of the Disney Boys' wives as a front. The Weasel was point man and protector, packager and enforcer. There was a story circulated about a mule that went south on a deal and tried to freelance by jumping on another flight. They found said mule hanging in the stall of a men's room three inches off the toilet seat.

But to my knowledge it was just a bedtime story. And Jack wanted to jump into this one with both his feet, not satisfied running errands and doing some scut work for the Boys. He wanted a nest egg they would give him for services rendered and to be made a partner. It was as if he was homing in on my thoughts, seeking my wavelength or his fucking ears were burning as my phone rang and I knew it was he.

"Remy?"

"Yes, Jack. What's up?" I asked in a tired voice.

"Did you see Elihu?"

"I did. We watched the Super Bowl until Mona's tits pushed me out the front door."

He laughed. "Mona there in her black Tura kit?"

"As per usual. What's up? I'm trying to sleep. Are you still in L.A.?"

"I am. But I'm on a PSA flight tomorrow."

"I'm working or I'd pick you up."

"No worries, I'll take the Airporter into the 'Loin and get home that way."

"How's Clovis?"

"Nervous."

"He was born nervous."

He laughed, "Isn't that no shit? Right, see you tomorrow."

There was a pregnant pause; I could feel him wrestling with it.

"Remy…did you talk to Elihu about me?"

"No, I was watching the game." And I hung up. I could imagine him with the Weasel in Lima and just felt really bad. Not a good image.

I know. I was the last guy they sent down there.

Chapter 8

The Weasel was well named. When I found out his real name by accident, it didn't make any difference. My adventures with him aren't a good memory. Hunter S. Thompson couldn't have dreamt him up no matter the amount of narcotics or booze he could consume. Small, wiry and dark eyes bugged like the guy in the 3-D glasses ads on the back of comic books with his affected Buddy Holly rims. He had partial uppers and removed them when he ate and had the disgusting habit of laying them out on the table no matter the caliber of restaurant, maître de hotels throwing him a jaundiced eye.

Clovis told me a story about when they were in a coffee shop on Kuhio, which was a typical Weasel eatery; hookers, drag queens, sailors —-the works. Anyway, he placed his partial on the table as per his habit and was so engrossed in the action in the coffee shop the waitress scooped up his teeth and into the garbage they went. When he was done eating, leaning back and enjoying his coffee and a cigarette he realized his teeth were gone. It took every ounce of self-control not to pull the piece he always carried and shoot the hapless waitress. After 45 minutes of dumpster diving he and Clovis finally gave up. Pissed off he took it out on a random bum sending the poor soul to the hospital.

His real name was Arthur Berberian. He came from a good family in Fresno who were in agriculture. After that I didn't know shit about him except that after Lima I never wanted to see him again. I almost killed him at the hotel and he hadn't forgotten it either. Picturing Arthur the Weasel and Jack together made sleep impossible. I would talk to him tomorrow night when he had settled down and I was done at work, better yet just have him meet me when Calloway came in, and eat downtown so I could get up and leave if he pissed me off, but not before warning him of any such ideas as carrying weight for these guys.

Chapter 9

Corky asked me straight off, "Did you kill any gooks?" He was one of the Disney Boys. They all had *those* names, 1950's nicknames like Corky, Spin, Moochie, Skinny and Sparky. They were teenagers when I was a kid in my coonskin watching Davy and Mike Fink race in their keelboats on TV. They were already in hotrods sporting DA's and chinos with Chippewa boots and Chesterfields rolled up in their sleeves. And they were already established outlaws. When I got back from my tours I was 22. Francois had told them he met me in L.A. and said I had *stones*, and when Clovis was back in their good graces he was more than happy to 'loan' me out. I was working for Dominic and then I was also working for them. I had access to the dispensary at Treasure Island as a vet and there was a guy who worked in the pharmacy that owed the Boys large amounts of cash for some degenerate reason above my pay grade but he could get his mitts on morphine and pharmaceutical coke and that's all they gave a shit about. And I was the guy to pick it up and deliver it. I had to actually make an appointment to meet this guy and set things up. The Boys were that meticulous in their execution. Easy day. And when I drove to Marin County to the designated bar in Mill Valley, I finally met the D-Boys in the flesh.

They were these rugged, good-looking dudes that resembled all the surfers I had known in Southern Cal; healthy and sun-kissed, laid back and unconcerned. But they also had this edge…this deadness in their eyes that spoke to no empathy or warmth, no memory of pleasure and no happy endings. On closer inspection you could make out the lines around their mouths, early vestiges of crow's feet under their tans. Their watches were Oyster Perpetuals, Cartier, Tag Heuer and the rings had real jewels. The casual pullovers expensive and slacks sported sharp nice creases. Corky was the only one in jeans, 501's faded to perfection, moccasins and a well-worn Van Huesen shirt, his Saint Christopher medal visible; the patron saint of all surfers.

"Did you kill any gooks?"

I didn't answer and sitting with my back to the door around these guys I felt like I was back on point in the platoon. I looked over my shoulder, catching the waitress's eye and nodded at the beers. He continued.

"Francois said you didn't even blink when he looked at you." One of the others, Moochie, laughed.

"Maybe he was scared shitless," and the others laughed. I lit a cigarette. "Fuck, you don't say much." The laughter died then.

The waitress brought the round and the one called Spin whistled, "Damn, he didn't say shit and we all got a fresh longneck," He eyed me as I paid for the round, "Francois may be a crazy motherfucker but he can pick them. You sure you're related to Clovis?"

They all laughed again.

"Yes." I said. Then took a drink.

"Yes what?" asked Corky.

"I killed a few." I stared at him until he looked away.

"Well, alright then." He looked at the others. "So there…you have something for us?"

"I do."

The one called Sparky finally spoke, "Okay, we'll finish these and you follow us. Follow the blue mustang." They all had separate cars, and I was in Elihu's old '59 Speedster that he loaned for this. While I fell in behind the Mustang, they fell in behind me. They were that careful. We drove up 1 towards Stinson Beach and the Mustang disappeared up a steep driveway and I followed. The house was a huge A-Frame that was in front of an old barn that was fenced in, housing a couple of horses. Chickens squawked out of the way, shaking their wings. Parking behind the blue car, I was firmly boxed in by the others as they came to stops. By this time the chickens had settled down and were just clucking outside the Porsche's open window. I got out slowly, walked to Corky and handed him the keys.

"In the trunk."

He smiled and laughed, "Man, brother, we trust you. You can open the boot yourself." Looking around I could see Spin had a hand behind him and I knew he was holding a piece, so I opened the trunk and stepped back, not reaching inside. Just then a petite brunette, her tank top pulled up and a baby at her tit appeared on the porch.

"Are you all staying for dinner?" she yelled, her tone exasperated.

Fucking ridiculous scene. Corky yelled at her to open some wine as Spin placed the gun inside his waistband in plain view of me. Corky pulled the box out of the trunk and we all started towards the house.

"Hey, no hard feelings, man…but you know…" He smiled.

Smiling back I knew. I knew I could never trust any of them for a New York second.

Doc Krinberg

Chapter 10

Jack walked up the hill from the Airporter Bus drop off in the 'Loin. He must've been just plain full of beans to power up to Pine Street, not jumping the cable car on Powell. I still had an hour until Calloway but luckily Dominic was gone and I was playing solitaire in the office when he walked in, with his cargo bag.

"What the fuck, Jack...I thought you were getting in earlier and then we'd meet for dinner?"

He dropped the case and sat across from me. "Nah, it was tough getting out of bed with Francine, and well you know. You've been there, done that." He laughed and took a cigarette from the pack lying on the desk.

"Just once, and never again. You don't smoke plain ends."

"I smoke yours. So?"

"So what? I'm still working."

"Yea, I see that. Queen on black king. Or in your case," he smiled lewdly, " Greek on black queen...still dating that *mavros?*" I looked at him. Everyone was curious about her, like a new attraction at the movies. Jack was always talking about black girls...what they were like, how they fucked, tasted, but had never been with one yet. He exhaled loudly, "Like some guys like to be tied up or ass-fucked, you like that exotic cooze, *adelfos*...its your fetish."

He went into shock when he first met Sylvia, and it wasn't lost on her. 'Greek thing?' she had asked. I avoided his inquiries and Jack being Jack went for the lowest denominator; too many Filipinas and Vietnamese girls when I was in the marines had ruined me for white women.

"Yes Jack. You're absolutely right."

The tone of voice made him redirect, "So how is that clown Elihu? Still pulling his Reginald Van Gleason sthick?"

I had to laugh at that. Elihu was always the standard blue blood that for all our sakes helped out the rest of us sweaty masses. He was our white savior. One night he lectured us on the onslaught of Laotian refugees and their predilection for hunting stray canines or those left unattended in Golden Gate Park. The police, according to Eli, discovered an underground cache of skinned dogs, or as he euphemistically termed them 'barking lobsters'. But he did have a healthy fear of the Disney Boys and of Francois as well. It seemed everyone feared Francois, and that was a healthy reflex. When I first moved up the coast and started school I got lonely and hit him up for one of his girls, as I didn't need some lovey-dovey thing. I bought him a beer when we met and traded the usual sea stories and service bullshit; this Gunny was an asshole, this Gunny was good people, the Island versus Pendleton, this shitbird 2nd looey deserved to be fragged, FTN (Fuck the Navy) and so on. Francois must've attended a lot of Office Hours, non-judicial punishment, as he went up and down the ranks in his career starting in the late 40's to avoid a jail sentence in Honolulu. Then, after Lebanon, he was done and back in Hawaii started being who he is. So he would fuck with me because I had made buck sergeant and a recon queen with my jump wings and scuba bubble, all in jest. Then he took me to one of his houses and told the mama-san there if I ever showed up to green light me, no charge. And so for the last few years I would make it a point to meet him at a roadhouse on old Bayshore he liked and buy him a few beers and he would rattle on about the Corps, Lebanon, and more importantly the Disney Boys and why you never fucked with them. I never got the vibe *he* was scared of them but he knew as much that to stay healthy, you didn't cross them.

The older he got, the more he spread out and really looked like one of those seriously heavy islanders. His ankles disappeared and his head got as big as a shitcan, his neck fused to his jaws. His hair was turning grey, as grey as his lifeless European eyes. He could've been married and putting five kids thru school for all I knew and probably would never know. We were all that much a mystery to one another as we kept our other private lives behind that wall we all maintained. Anyway, I wasn't interested in getting married, having kids and a house in Petaluma. Francois' houses were good enough for me. Then.

Jack…

We went to dinner and hung out awhile. There was a bar on Jones that he liked so we made it there.

"I really want to do this, Remy. I want that reward. I've got some investment ideas and this would make it solid. The broker I've been talking to has some serious portfolios."

I leaned over so we could be more discreet. "It isn't that easy. It's like having your skin removed and all your nerve endings exposed. And the guy you travel with, the connection that makes the purchase is a fucking nightmare in his own right. Lots of stress. You don't know if you're going to be taken off, killed or held down and goat fucked. It's insane. " I flicked my cigarette ash on the floor and remembered the night the Weasel and I took possession of the product. "Its not worth the effort."

He screwed his mouth to one side, pulling his brows down, "C'mon…you did it. Seriously, I need this cuz. Clovis broached it."

I pictured Jack and his hair trigger temper with the Weasel and it made me queasy. Jack, unable to stop once he started snorting up and the amount, the sheer bulk of all the loose blow left over when it gets packaged is all fair game and untraceable. It spoke to pure dereliction. And the way the Weasel used that extra blow…how would Jack handle *that* scene?

Once we had purchased the keys, the Weasel and I were inseparable; the crystalline ball and chain as unmovable as the Hulk. I didn't see Jack living thru that. "Remy, please, help me out on this. Clovis won't go and Elihu would never. I can't ask them directly man, you know that. It's almost a Masonic thing…they have to ask you. Clovis did and I've gotta be recommended. "

"Then why not have Clovis do it."

"He did already. He called Elihu again this morning before I left. Elihu wants to hear it from you."

"Fucker, you spent all this morning blowing Clovis…you weren't with Francine." I laughed.

He smiled. "I was with her until I woke up. Yes, I had to take that fucking part Okie asshole to eat at Ollie Hammonds for breakfast. Even Meredith backed me up and you know what a bitch she can be. You ever notice she still uses all that Yardley shit from the 60's…swinging London shimmery lip stick stuff?"

I barely paid attention to her and Clovis when growing up or since my hitch was done and I moved up north. We did everything by pay phone.

"I don't know, Jack, to be honest I don't think you and this guy will mesh very well. I foresee a clash of personalities, not unlike the demise of Martin & Lewis, but with two murderous psychos instead."

"And the other people we deal with aren't?" He was right there, to a point, but I also felt I was pulling a trigger on him by talking to Elihu.

"Jesus, Remy, do I have to blow you, too?" A woman down the row of booths from us on the opposite side of the aisle was staring at us when he said that. I laughed, but not a real laugh. All I wanted to do was go home to my bed, pull Sylvia down on me and forget all this insanity. I looked at my cousin Jack, I felt very tired.

I sighed. "Your karma. Don't fuck it up."

Doc Krinberg

Chapter 11

"So if you're Greek, how did you get a name like Remy? Isn't that French?" Sylvia asked.

"It's a very lame Hollywood style story." I hated telling it.

"Well?"

I went into the kitchen of my flat to get the bottle. She was sitting up in bed with one of my sweaters on, as I had my window open as usual. I had started to drink cognac when I was at Pendleton. My Gunny Sergeant's only drink and when at his house with his Okinawan wife, we would drink and play chess. And drink. And listen to 'Trane, Horace Silver, Miles Davis, Bird.

I walked back into the bedroom, putting the bottle on the nightstand and handing her a small rounded snifter. "Well?" She asked again. I held up the bottle.

"My parents had tried for years after the war to conceive, but no dice. One weekend in '48 they just said to hell with it, drove up the coast nice and leisurely, as my dad had taken the following Monday off. They drove all the way up here to the City, stopping along the way at those fruit stands on 99. On a lark, they lucked into a room at the Fairmount on a cancellation. Relaxed, they ordered room service and my dad asked the bellman to recommend a liquor and it was this." I showed her the label. "And after that weekend, I was the result, so they figured it was the Remy

Martin."

She laughed. "And named you Remy! Is your middle name 'Martin'?"

"Nooo…I got a traditional name for that. Alexio." I poured two glasses. "At least it wasn't Gus or Harry…or worse, Spiro. All standard Greek names."

She twitched her nose, "Spiro? Like Agnew?"

"Yes."

"Good thing they didn't drink Cutty Sark. What's your cousin's name who lives here? Jack? Not very Greek. Don't remember a Jack in my mythology class."

"His real name is Costas. To get along with other kids he started using Jack. His brother Nico became Nick. See, there was this newly arrived Israeli kid named Ari, and he was mercilessly needled, even by other Jewish kids until one day he beat the shit out of one and told everyone from then on to call him Bob."

"How sad. So much for the melting pot theory."

"Well, we Mediterranean folk don't have the luxury of WASPY surnames like you all do." I teased. "Where did Sylvia come from? Old relation?"

"Not as romantic as a lost weekend of drinking and sex, just an old friend of my mother's. And all you Mediterranean folk weren't previously owned by luxurious WASPY people." She said drily.

"Ouch."

There was a silence as we drank.

"Wow!" She rasped.

"Yea, takes getting used to. Like with us. Little by little." I meant it.

"You really see this happening? Hmmm…just because you've eaten bbq?" She smiled.

"Yea...so why did you go for this?"

She sipped the cognac slowly, thought a minute, "It just felt right. No more, no less. And I liked the Stones ever since I saw them on the T.A.M.I. Show, even *after* watching James Brown. You're kinda this Greek Keith Richards...better teeth, shorter hair and after that first night of sparking on Union Street I just feel damn good with you." She looked towards my window. "Remy, have you ever seen that big silk thing, like a sleeping bag up in the corner of your window frame?"

I looked up. "Looks like he's sleeping for the winter."

"Nasty, I hate spiders. When it finally wakes up, it'll be looking for trouble and its appetite will be voracious." I thought about that. I knew guys in the Corps who were like that when they woke up. Some guys on the line as well. One day, tucked away nice and cozy, the next they were killing machines.

I got up, dropped my robe, and walked back to the kitchen. Over my shoulder I said, "And you like Greek food too."

"Nasty man." I loved her laugh.

Doc Krinberg

Chapter 12

That moment stuck in time, that one pivotal thing that everyone relegates to fate; the Rubicon moment. And everyone usually wants this moment back, the words reversed into our mouths, the match backing away from the fuse. Not happening! Felt it in the second I called Elihu and told him to make Jack's dream come true. I didn't realize they wanted a body in the mix by early spring. They had already set it up and just needed a mule. I didn't know it but they were on the verge of asking me again at a higher return after I said it would never happen and if I saw the Weasel again I would kill him.

The body they *did* have turned out to be just that; a body. He croaked right after New Year from an overdose and after a group sigh of relief that it happened before and not during. There was pressure on Clovis to talk to me but he refused knowing too well I meant what I said. Over the years he and I came to an understanding and he didn't speak for me nor speak against me. We might be blood but it ended there. Jack, well, not so much with so much shared history.

But this dead runner was a game changer. He was also a friend of one of the Disney Boys and it was all ready and smoothed down the line. People were aware, bribes had been paid and they needed a shot of juice from a run. It was a must go thing, so Jack stepped up into that and after I hung up the phone with Elihu and rolled into Sylvia's backside, I already regretted it.

Chapter 13

Since meeting Sylvia I stopped dropping by Francois' place in Daly City, but he and I still kept in touch. He was a guy who would take umbrage at a social slight and act as if it were nothing, but it would burn inside him slowly and finally one day just implode. I found out years later it was the reason he was going to scotch my cousin in L.A. Clovis had leaned on Francois to help him out when he married Meredith in Waikiki intimating that he wished Francois to be his best man, but he had already designated that chore to Elihu. Francois, who had connections all over the island had these beautiful leis made and furnished all the floral arrangements. At the wedding he saw what the deal was and very softly told Clovis the price of the floral arrangements and leis and expected payment. Clovis, of course welshed on him and only after years Francois decided he would just kill him for that slight! Crazy shit…he just held it in forever. So, I still dropped in and had a beer.

"You old school, Remy. I 'preciate you dropping by to socialize. What da fuck's wrong with yo cuz Clovis? Is it cuz he's part Okie? When we together in da kine I show him and Eli all manner of scams. Dem two could take a boosted Amex card and buy up over half of Kalakau they had such a smooth line of tourist shit. But he got no soul. He's so haole." And he shook his head, and then changing the subject, " Dis girl must be damn fine for you not to fuck Lorna no more." Lorna had been my regular, very sweet and sadly only 9th grade educated. Most of the girls had been runaways or dropouts. Sylvia asked me if I were 'dating' at all and saying no I felt was an honest answer.

    I never made any attempt to defend Clovis. Or Jack for that matter. Francois had met Jack and while liking him initially felt he had a little too much arrogance; too full of himself. Jack worked on Van Ness at an imported fine car firm as a sales rep and moved a lot of cars. When I was sweating bullets in MCRD he was hopping cars at Scandia's on the strip and making good bank boosting whatever he could, and the entire crew was cutthroat thieves fighting over rights to rummage thru whatever dash board they could. In those days people left tons of dope, or even cash stuffed into the glove box, under the seats. Eight track cassette players were also fair game and the turn over at the valet parking was pretty high volume, yet Jack seemed to have a solid in, probably snitching out others who had taken the rap for shit he boosted. Jack seem to own this slippery skin that just allowed him to operate in high-risk environments and survive. But he also had loose lips and told one of the girls some shit to look cool disparaging Francois, and talking shit about him wasn't a good idea. He knew Jack had referred to him as a 'fucking moke' once when he had used two of his girls at a party for out of town buyers It also reflected badly on me as I had set it up to get the girls. I wondered how many years that slight would take before Francois just walked up to him and bitch slapped him into next week, or worse? Those two were big boys and I learned that stepping in front of one wasn't a good thing. When you made your bed with this crowd, you had better sleep in it.

    I had to 'drop' something off for Dominic, as he wasn't feeling well the day after I green lighted Jack for Peru. I was down near the airport and played a dime to see if Francois was good for a beer. We met after I connected with a guy in a beautiful grey flannel suit from L.A. who talked all 'Joisey' around a toothpick and complained he hated coming up to 'FruitsVille'. I gave him a peace sign as I left him and met Francois.

"So, your cuz Jack gonna make da trip?" First thing he said when he pushed my beer across the table at me.

"Jesus, does everyone know? Joe Bavarresco and the Perfect 36 in on it too?" I asked sarcastically.

"Hey, dese guys are pulling chocks and getting ready for the big one. Dis run gonna bring in some heavy jeedas." He drank looking at me, " You smart never to go again. They prob'ly have a picture of you somewhere down there. Not like da cops don't know."

I was quiet. Thinking of it made me feel bad. My only good memory of that trip for me was the surfing. He broke the silence; "You think Jack get along with da Weasel?"

"Hey, he's a born salesman, and probably end up selling the Weasel a car." But I didn't believe that.

Francois laughed, " Dat Weasel is a funny guy. You know his ohana is rich, own a bit of farmland in Central Valley, but still da way he is. Da only ting my fatha gave me was dese grey eyes." The older Francois got, the more he opened up. It was he who dropped the Weasel's real name, and the fact he came from money. He repeated it to me, maybe forgetting he had already mentioned it. Or just the thought of rich kids becoming criminals, he didn't seem to grasp why. It was no matter to me, why the Weasel was the way he was. I knew him as a psycho with a stutter. I can still see him asking the barely teen girls at the beach in Lima 'Where's the p-p-party?' He would sit on the beach, watching me. In Miraflores, Punte Hermosa and Waikiki beach and Makaha, surf beaches named after Oahu. It was a pleasure not to have to surf wearing rubber like off Baker's Beach so I took the boat to Comotal and enjoyed a couple of hours without him but he was pissed. I said hey, if you want me to have a good beard, I have to play the part. I was carrying it home in one of two boards I travelled with. One was waiting for me there, a duplicate of mine with the estimated same weight when full if they checked, that we set up before we left, getting filled and reglassed. The trick was the travel bag. Heavy going down, light when coming back. I even wore puka shells around my neck; a gift from Francois himself. The fucking Weasel. Sitting on that beach in his street clothes, no matter how hot. It was winter in California and semi summer down south and yet he sat in a windbreaker and jeans, a canvas porkpie on his head.

"All I gotta say is he better not fuck dis one up. I told dem I got trust in you, but dey knew you wouldn't. Dey need da Weasel and dey also know you'd plant him somewhere. Fuck it."

And we finished our drinks.

Chapter 14

Sylvia liked going to the Mabuhay Gardens and was interested in the punk scene as well as rock. She was like this contradiction in many ways that I supposed was my *issue* of perception and stereotyping. She laughed at my obviously quizzical look when she alerted me to the Sex Pistols at Winterland. She added with amusement to pile on my obviously poor misconception, '…hey Remy, I don't even own a wig'. So, the Mabuhay, which was a tame Filipino restaurant by day, became a serious counter culture cattle call at night. It was kitty-corner from City Lights bookstore on Broadway and she introduced me to a few things in there as well and I peeled back another layer of this woman. She started talking to me about my tastes and values and it was really the first time I confronted myself in what attracted me, inspired me. I had never been so self reflective and it was weird to me. I was a mile wide and an inch deep and she called me on it. Even during boot camp and subsequent duty I just internalized things. I was open to anything but I didn't discuss it or roll it around like navel contemplation. It also made me take measure of my *other* life, the not so legal aspects. But I just rationalized and let it go. She would joke with me and say I had skipped the entire white hippie self-awareness and mind expansion classes. I wondered if I had squandered an intellectual episode and reflected on my old Gunny turning me onto Nietzsche, talking chess techniques and Capoblanco's games at Pendleton. I'd rolled that one quote of his, *"There are no beautiful surfaces without a terrible depth"* and I understood that from jump street; *that* was how I saw things. That was my philosophy. If you couldn't hack the pressure, don't go deep. Only that terrific dark, cold water could support any beauty. My alter-life was that terrible depth but I didn't feel it. I just lived in it.

So what did I miss? It was obviously a lot more than I realized. I told her the Marines were my university and the war was my graduate school. She asked if I was bitter and I wasn't. I wasn't really anything and when I admitted it she was surprised. I didn't meet her expectations of hard-boiled pissed off grunt. I just didn't think of it when I left. I never admitted it to anyone, but I actually felt comfortable there. It was the same as when I picked up something for Elihu, or delivered a paper bag with cash for Dominic. It was a natural reflex. She walked up to the line but never crossed it in ascertaining whether or not I was a life taker, and I never offered that puzzle piece. She didn't press me balls to the wall like Corky. She never asked about the two star shaped scars I had on my flank either, with corresponding scars on my back. But, she had a way of making me look back, in my own private way, and I had to look at that younger me, the one in jungle ripstops; look him in the face. When I did, it was just like a photograph of someone I vaguely knew.

That weekend after the Super Bowl was Pro Bowl in Honolulu and had it not been the high tourist season and so last minute I almost wanted to jump to the islands, grab Sylvia and get away from all these characters, intrigues and Jack's impending run. I knew there wouldn't be a vacant room or a rent-a-car available so I quashed that idea but I needed a respite from the City. I also had a crazy idea of driving to L.A. and introducing Sylvia to my folks, but turned that off as fast as it entered my head. I just had this fleeting image of my mother's eyes and that was enough. In line with some of my reflective moments, I had to agree that they knew nothing about me. I was this kid that grew up there and shared that house, but for how I turned out, my experiences, there was nothing. My seeing Sylvia would be like hooking them up to car batteries and throwing the switch! Or perhaps I wasn't giving them enough credit. But my dad had stopped voting Democratic since 1968. So that was there as well. They had finally moved from our old house off Crescent Heights and Sawyer to Westchester, near Lincoln Blvd. in their own personal white flight while Jack and Nick's parents went to South Beverly Hills.

Sylvia had only her mother left and her migration to the Western Addition from their home in Portrero Hill was needed when she enrolled in her courses at USF and she was hired at the Med Center as well. The other factor being her mother became extremely religious and had, like many in the People's Temple, become a donor to the American Communist Party in the last few years, and now she disappeared to Guyuna and Jonestown, selling her modest home on the hill and giving all the proceeds to the church. Sylvia had fought her on that and lost, receiving one letter from her since her departure. I got all this that first night at the Cantata, down on Union Street. It had class even though it was considered a fern bar. They had shot a scene from 'Bullitt' there when McQueen and a very young and hot Jackie Bissett go out to hear some jazz and eat dinner to establish how hip they are, as if McQueen had to establish *that*. And so I rode my bike there that night and walking in found her sitting at the bar drinking a greyhound.

She looked fine.

Those first glimpses of people you're attracted to, that photo image you keep forever, that was one of them. She was one of those women that could look deadly in even the simplest of clothes. She had a black, sleeveless collared button down blouse top, these spectacular white jeans, and her feet in tanned open toed sandals. On the back of the barstool was a small pearl colored Chinese coat with a silent crane in the folds. Her hair was still just kissing her shoulders and she wore it relaxed and soft. Since Union Square she had only added a hint of lipstick. I walked to her and seeing my jacket and pushed back hair shook her head.

"I should've guessed you had a bike," she teased. And we sat at that long elegant wood bar for three more hours, our stools turned to each other, knees touching. I froze my ass off, even though it was summer riding back to the Sunset-Cole Valley district while she huddled behind me in my coat, and later asked why in hell I lived up three narrow flights of stairs, but was pleasantly surprised when I opened the door and turned on the lights.

"Very nice...very, Spartan? You live alone and keep it this clean? Can you train my roommate?" She took off my coat. "Yes, it's the marine in you. This is a giant footlocker and you just keep it squared away." I let her walk around the small living room and investigate. I had a couple of Gaugain reprints framed over my small couch against the wall. My drinking buddy Gunnery Sargent turned me onto him. I had always felt a weird attachment to them since returning from overseas.

"Want something to drink?" I took my coat from her shoulders and hung it up.

"Ice water?" She walked into the bathroom and flicked on the light. "Hmm, the lids down. Were we anticipating anything?" She smiled, enjoying the game.

"No, I just like to squat, but don't tell anyone."

"Am I going to find anything in here hanging behind the door... perhaps a G-string?"

"Only mine." And we went on like that until we started undressing as we kissed.

Chapter 15

One day I got a call from Elihu and he asked me to fall by his place after work the next week. I figured he had an odd job he wanted done but it was far weirder.

When I finally showed up at his house later in the next week he was listening to this Cuban big band stuff from the 40's he was enamored with; Alberto Ruiz specifically. He was always off on some esoteric twist whether it was music or collecting meerschaum pipes. He would crawl through antique shops and estate sales seeking the old carved pipes. Then the next week it would be Commando Cody & The Lost Planet Airman and exotic stickpins. I always wondered where the non-working rich spent their time, and Elihu like the Weasel certainly didn't have to be outlaws but they just were. Anyway, he finally turned down the music and offered me a beer. I had a feeling it was going to be about Jack, but it wasn't.

"Are you going to want to invest anything in the upcoming events? I'm sure you could make a solid contribution, Remy. You've always struck me as more the ant than the grasshopper." The thought of investing in the upcoming run to Lima hadn't even crossed my mind. In the first place, I wanted as little as possible to do with any of it, already regretting vouching for Jack, and secondly I also didn't wish to have anything traceable to me if it went tits up.

"NO. Nothing. I'm strictly hands off this one." I had no intentions of putting a penny in. "I had no idea it was even going on until around the time Jack started nagging me and you asked me to vouch for him. Two, no one even thought to ask me until *now*. And I have other plans. Three, I'm good with the hand I'm holding." I was looking into his eyes, as I talked trying to figure out where he was coming from. " So why are you asking? Don't these guys have investors from tennis shoe pimps to Montgomery Street sharpies already lined up?"

"Yes, all true. I was just curious. You don't have any dealings with Mr. Berberian do you?"

I laughed, "C'mon Eli, you should know better. We haven't even seen each other since I flipped him off at LAX after that trip. Why?"

"He sort of went dark for awhile in the last couple of weeks. No one could get a line on him. I know you hang out with Francois time to time (how in the fuck did *he* know that?)…Has he mentioned seeing the Weasel?"

"He hasn't mentioned it and listen, you fuckers named him didn't you, gave him that nickname, so maybe he's just living up to it." I took one of his cigarettes. He always had those fat French ones that were extremely harsh and had a name I couldn't say. "Is his powder causing some disturbance?"

"In a way, yes. It was as if he just vanished for a bit, and then poof! Out of nowhere he returned. He's enroute already to set things up. Just hoping perhaps you could shed some light on it." He took one of his smokes, lighting it mechanically.

"Why didn't you just ask Francois?"

"Because basically, you're the only person who he talks to and actually *talks* to, if you understand."

"And how do all of you fuckers know that?"

Elihu smiled. "We know a lot, obviously not everything, but we get around. Didn't you have a finger on all the men in your platoon? Wanted to know what they were about, how they'd do in a fight?" I had to agree, but it creeped me out.

"Well, has anyone asked the Weasel? And maybe you all need to back off and leave me in the dark. There are people I associate with who may not appreciate your knowing them." I had the Teamster guys in mind.

"No one did. It isn't like he's *here*."

I started to put the whole conversation down to pre-run paranoia. They were all ouch cubes of spent nerves prior to embarking on this deal. And I had to wonder how much they invested in this one. It seemed like it was a bigger too-do than mine.

And it all rode on Jack's shoulders.

Sometimes Elihu was like snakes in a frying pan; repulsive yet fascinating in his gyrations and predicament. I understood why he really asked me if I wished to invest in this clambake. He wanted to bail! The disappearance of the Weasel had spooked him and he wanted to pull chocks and flee. He would take my money, probably a thousand which was chicken feed to him, hand it over to the Disney Boys and get his back. The silly part is he never even needed the fucking money *or* the deal. I almost laughed in his face when I figured it out, but I kept mum and just studied him. He had this repertoire of fidgeting he would go thru when he was wrapped tight. Fucking Elihu. No wonder he and Clovis were tight.

"Well," I announced, slapping my knees and standing up, "I have some shit to do. Kites to fly, fish to fry." I smiled.

I looked down at Elihu and he wasn't paying attention to me, just worrying one of his fingernails in between his teeth. I told nobody in particular I would see my way out and left his parlor, down the long hallway to the front door. Elihu's place was one of the finer old houses near Union and Filbert. I had thought of calling Sylvia as she was on the way home but decided to keep my own counsel that night. I was admiring the wainscoting and woodwork in the passageway when Mona ambushed me. She had come out of a small water closet near the main foyer and about gave me a heart attack.

"Remy! What're you doing?" She whispered. She turned in her black Tura kit for a light blue terrycloth robe that made her blue-black hair shimmer, as if it were a reflecting pool.

"I'm leaving. Be good." And I turned away. A firm and very iron like set of fingers pinched my shoulder—no pain but an attention getter.

"Remy, Elihu is scared of something. You know what?" She peeked down the empty passageway towards his parlor. I could hear the rhythm of the Cuban music again.

"No Mona, I haven't a clue…do you? What do you think?"

She peeked again, "He can't keep his dick hard last couple of weeks and he's doing a ton of blow."

I almost laughed out loud at her description of Elihu's fear meter. "Maybe something you need to take up with him." And before I could move her hand was cupping my crotch, pinning me inside my jeans. She moved closer and pushed those big tits into me. She smiled.

"You're not scared."

"I just have a different reaction to things that *do* scare me." And I backed up and went to the door. She had opened the robe, smiling. It had been one thing to see those coaster sized tips thru black tee shirts and sweaters but it was quite another to see them like that. I looked down. Why are the wild ones always hairless?

I went out the door looking like I had stuffed a magazine down my jeans. Elihu must be really scared not to erect in *that* house.

Chapter 16

A couple of week's later Dominic was beating round the bush over something. He would start to say things then stop, cursing himself out. A couple of times he would engage me in talk and then say 'phooey' and walk away. Whatever the jungles of Guadalcanal or Tarawa did to his jaw, it was pretty active as he looked as if he were chewing hard over a full count in the bottom of the ninth. I often wondered if I had any weird shit inside me after leaving South East Asia being pretty much a bush Marine. The bar girls on Magsaysay Street in Olangapo were way more dangerous at times than shit we encountered in the line ever was! Gunny Hicks made sure our Doc had the proper dope to take care of us all once we returned from R&R so we wouldn't be sneaking off from duty to attend sick call, our dicks dripping like broken faucets. Luckily, I survived all that but often wondered if I'd got something that would erupt years later. The jungles were mighty fucked up for those who visited and not indigenous, or had the bad luck to wander thru a defoliated area.

He finally blurted it out when I came back from the Greek's down the hill on Taylor Street with a sandwich. "Here's your sandwich Dominic." Every Friday I would drop down there to get him a tongue sandwich.

"Sit down damnit, Remy!" He snapped.

So I sat and waited. I watched his jaw work hard and I just settled in my Doc Brown's cream soda.

"The Union bosses are making some changes. They want to move some people around and do some upkeep at some of the other garages…personnel, and all that bullshit."

"Okay." I just started eating. No sense in wetting myself.

"They want me out at the airport. They were thinking of bringing some jamoke in here, some guy not even from the City. I was fucking born here in North Beach. I told them to fuck that noise. I told them to promote you and have you run the operation, and anyway, they know you…all of them favors you done me, all them deliveries and odds and ends, they know you for six years. They trust you. So I says, 'Remy can handle it, he's young and smart and he was a combat fucking marine.' So, the garage is yours. You get a big raise and you also get a vote. You're smart Remy. You know which guys to hire and which are troubles. I don't understand these young guys anymore and I rely on you. So…it's yours. You get more *benefits* too."

I didn't know what to say. I just looked at him and ate.

He continued, "The airport is closer to home for me and all I gotta do is show up and say what the fuck and then go home. So, can do, kid?"

I bit into a pepperoncini and threw the stem into the shitcan. What the hell was I supposed to say? I'd been pretty much running it for the last 2 years and anyway it could be an outlet from any more relations from my 'other' work." I smiled at Dominic.

'Sounds good to me."

He let out a sigh of relief, "Damn, I didn't know you'd go for it and tell me to piss up a rope. Good!" He was relieved at once, his jaw slowing down considerably.

So I sat there at the garage on Pine Street, my cousin's future was a plane ready to make the southbound run. I wondered if we shared the same thoughts when I made my trip there, as I sat waiting with my seatbelt on, dying for the smoking lamp to be lit and get a drink. I wondered how many seats and aisles would separate Mr. Arthur Berberian and my cousin Jack. Would he, like me, break down and peek around to find him? I thought about his score, how big and what role was he playing? He didn't surf like I did so how would they bring it back this time? Anyway, I'd find out in a month or so when he would pound on my door, flush and fat and taking me out, fill in all the dirty details and share *his* Weasel stories.

So I thought.

Doc Krinberg

Chapter 17

    They had just recaptured Ted Bundy after his jailbreak. Some clown had even written a song about him as if he were some fucking folk hero! It was mid-February and raining. Dominic hadn't as of yet shuffled off his Pine Street coil but he was packing things and gave me the keys to the kingdom. That same day I was reading about Bundy, this guy visits and he has 'union' all over him. Dominic asks me to shut the door and we all discuss the changing of the guard and a lot of other shit he was up to I didn't even know about and now it would all involve me. I'd made a mental note to ask one of the lawyers who stowed his heap in the garage about what sort of charges were territorial to money laundering.

    No matter what, it seemed as if I were born to be a criminal.

    The day dragged on and the rain just intensified. I was glad I had stowed my bike. It was a '73 Norton 850 Commando, tucked way back into the dry confines of the garage. I liked taking it out when Sylvia would hold me tightly and lay the side of her face on my back. I enjoyed that intimacy while hurling down Highway 1 somewhere south like Half Moon Bay running high. We would stop at a hotel there, drinking beer and listening to the gulls as they swooped in and out. She laughed the first time I called them 'flying rats.' I told her how the sailors at the bases would throw chicken bones at them as they would gobble them up, then take bets on which ones would choke and crash first. She would shake her head, and then tell me to stop and not tell her any military stories. I wouldn't even know why I would. I often asked myself what was I thinking?

Calloway called, said he was running late due to the rain, and I said to take his time, no hurry. The shift change went smooth, the older full time guys off and the younger part time students on at night. It gave me impetus to talk to the evening shift guys about Dominic going and my taking the garage. Since Calloway was late, this gave some of the night shift guys some spine and started regaling me with Calloway complaints. I didn't realize the night guys wanted to murder him!

Seems Mr. Calloway had some nefarious friends and one of the guys said there was money changing hands at times. I asked if drugs or gambling; what was their impression, I mean I knew he fucking gambled. One guy, the most vocal was putting himself thru SFSU said he thought it was dope.

Fucking dope. It made the world go around. The thought of Calloway dealing sort of blew me away, and dealing now out of MY garage? If Dominic had known, he would've had his legs broken or worse…find him tits up in the rip-rap that's left of the Sutro Baths with a hole in the back of his head. I had nothing going on so decided to hang out and talk to Calloway about Dominic. He knew the general stuff but not some of the specifics, or those I could tell him and in Calloway's defense I couldn't rely solely on what some hemp-smoking hump said. I'd have to see it. The whole idea of it was sort of weird.

He came steaming in thru the rain and pulled his car down the main floor to the back wall. Later he would pull it back and use it, along with other cars to block off the entrance and up and down ramps until Shepard, the night man used his car to block it off as Calloway took off. Calloway had been on the evening shift for 5 years, since his discharge from the army.

"So how does it feel to be the second coming of Dominic?" He laughed, as he came towards me, tucking is work shirt in.

"I'll have to start chewing gum and working my jaw more." We both smiled. "Howza family?

And so we exchanged small talk and I assured him nothing was going to change, and how did he get along with the swing shift guys? Any problems? Calloway shook his head no, said they were great guys; no issues. And so there was that. I stayed into dinnertime and so decided to walk down to the Stockton Street tunnel overpass to eat at a Japanese place there down the block from Burritt Street. Then later, walk back and keep an eye on the garage for a bit. So tonight, I'd be the Continental Op and maybe kill two birds with one stone; make or break Calloway and thereby reinforce my position at the garage. One can never have enough security.

It was miserable even in my army-navy store pea coat I kept at the garage and the doorway across the street didn't offer much cover but it was totally shrouded in dark, far enough from the street light farther up Pine, and I discovered the night guys paid as little attention to it as we did during the day. I had stayed an extra hour on top of the hour I spent in pounding tempura shrimp, vegetables, Sapporo and warm sake. There was never too much action at night besides hotel guests, the legal people in the adjacent offices who worked late or some action was at the Bohemian Club and we would get the late guys who missed getting stalls at the Olympic Garage on Sutter. Tonight it was pretty dead in the pouring rain. Then a black Merc drove slow up the street and stopped in front of the down ramp driveway to the basement storage. It had smoked dark windows as it reflected the garage lights, but I was clueless as to the occupants from where I was. The window cracked slowly and a cigarette was flicked out in the rain. It just sat there peacefully, the exhaust barely visible.

Fucking Calloway, thirty-five years old, going bald and two kids at home came out of the garage carefully, looking over his shoulder and pulling his rain slicker over his head went directly to the passenger side of the Merc. I couldn't hear anything and it could've been his wife or a friend of his for all I knew then for some reason the driver's side window went down and a large head popped out and spat on the street and then it silently pulled back into the car.

Francois!

This was a conversation waiting to happen.

Chapter 18

Time ticked by. When you're just living it and have a pattern you fail to pay attention to what other people are up to. The Ides of March saw Vida Blue traded to the Giants for 7 players, which was a major deal in the Bay Area. Would be weird not to see him in an A's uniform. March 21 saw the city pass the Homosexual Bill of Rights for lack of a better definition. Harvey Milk had his victory.

And so my routine just rolled on. I usually got up at about five-thirty, if I wasn't hung over and sometimes did a little work on this old speedbag the guy on the 1st floor flat had hanging on his lanai. He was 75 and liked that it was getting some use and a little beat down on occasion. He had named it after his ex wife. Over the fence that was draped in thick wild black berries, in the next yard the older Chinese guys would start their Tai Chi as I was ending my workout. I would mop the sweat off myself and watch them glide thru their motions in silence, then climb the three floors to my flat. From that side of the building I could hear the N-Judah car sliding up her track on Irving Street like fingers up steel fret board. My phone was ringing when I got back inside. It was my father in a tense voice.

"What the hell are you doing up there, Remy?" I had to pause a second and did a minor freak out thinking my parents knew about Sylvia. Then I remembered Jack stopped in LA before heading down south and figured he had run his soup coolers.

"Not doing anything, Dad…just work." It sounded lame as I said it.

"Yes? That's it? You're not involved in your *kakourgos* cousin Costa's business?" First twinge and start of the sinking feeling. "Yes, your goddamn piece of shit cousin who's in jail in Central America for…drug trafficking!" I just shut my eyes. On the one hand relieved he was alive, and also that I knew it would happen. I just knew.

"So, Aunt Carmen and Uncle Gus called you?" My voice was steady and I tried to sound concerned.

"They were contacted by some guy in the State Department. The goddamn State Department!" Must've been a long night with D.C., three hours ahead of the Left Coast…'Hello Mr. and Mrs. Christopoulos? Your son is in jail in Panama. Have a nice day.'

My dad was white heat pissed off.

"Calm down, Pop. Can't get all crazy over this. At least he's been detained and not dead. We'll get him out." I sounded like I was talking outside of my body it all just felt so unreal.

"What do you mean *we* Remy? Tell me, did you know anything about his business?"

"Not *that* business, just his car business, Pop. We move in different circles." I started writing a few things down as I talked to make sure I had some of the facts straight. I could feel the heat incoming in his voice. This was a major fuck up. I looked at my watch. "Pop, I have to go to work. I'll call you later."

And that was it. I didn't have to inform anybody else. I was the last person to know. The Weasel would've called within the hour it happened and all and sundry would be hip to it. I had no stake in any of it with exception of being his relative, which meant nothing to these guys. If my Pop called this early in the morning, early morning/late night in Los

Angeles, then Jack must've dropped a couple of days ago. He'd be processed and then taken off to some facility. They would contact the embassy and then wait for some low level suit to show up, get all the info, see the passport and then finally Jack for verification, get prints maybe or anything pertinent and until then the Panamanians wouldn't of put a hand on him. But if he had given them any shit, and he started being Jack, they'd present him without a bruise and once the State guy left, beat the shit out of him and blame it on fellow prisoners.

    Good fucking morning!

Doc Krinberg

Chapter 19

I wanted to talk to the Weasel to get the full story, but then doubted I could get close without him pulling a piece for self-preservation. Francois might have the real story so decided to call him later for a meet. Calling Elihu would be a bust—he'd already be far too schizzed out to even maintain a normal conversation and calling Clovis wasn't smart. He may have a wired phone from who knows what bizarre shit he was up to at the time.

The problem was no one knew what Jack was saying—so I'm sure all the *Cognoscenti* were under the radar. One thing was for sure, the Weasel would've already contacted a lawyer, and probably a guy they kept on retainer down there for just such emergencies and he would advise Jack on what to do. They didn't just smuggle blow. They had their mitts in all manner of legal *and* criminal enterprises in regards to the southern hemisphere.

Jail in another country has far different protocols than being dropped state side. Here you have rights; there you just have your balls. In Latin America the balancing act of too little, or too many balls is more a ballet. Different levels of manliness…if you go Steve McQueen cool, they'll just beat you down, wear you out. If you become a helpful witness, they know you'll take an assfucking. It was something that called for a level head and discipline. Jack at times had neither. So his lawyer would start letting him know what he would need, his income, and how his people in the States could send it to him so the lawyer could disburse the funds to those who would help him survive. The country of Panama wasn't going to foot the bill. If Jack were a local who had no money, he would pretty much each shit daily. But a man with an income could live properly and start making some deals and connections. He could be the King, and find his Peter Marlowe. This stake, the lawyer and the set up would be part of the group's interest to get Jack on a steady footing, set up and comfortable, feeling secure. They wouldn't want him feeling like he were twisting in the wind and would name names to lighten his burden. And it would be relatively cheap to institute this foundation for him. But once settled, and once in the system, it would primarily fall to Jack's family and friends to start sending money to the lawyer to maintain his position, get him a contact for street food and so as not to die from intestinal parasites like the local fellows who ate only prison chow.

I tried to picture Jack taking the fall and it was hard for me. But no one was calling me, telling me, asking me to fly there and talk sense to him, so he must be standing up so far. I remember when I was drafted after failing to register at SMCC in a state of pure apathy and procrastination and went into the Marines he and I had a conversation before I got on the train for MCRD San Diego. He bought me a soda, took out a flask and poured some Old Forrester into the cup. He just shook his head and told me straight up he could never have someone get in his face like that, his frame of reference being Jack Webb in 'The D.I."

"Why didn't you join the navy? Best place to be during a land war against a country with a borrowed air force." He made sense, but I wanted to be in the war and I just couldn't explain it. "Jesus, Remy, just this summer you had your hair hitting your shoulders and were stoned to 'Disraeli Gears' and telling anyone who hadn't tuned you out that Clapton was God." I laughed at that memory. And also laughed at memory of my drill sergeant screaming in my face '…where are you from, defecation reflex?' So, I had to wonder how he was holding out. I didn't need anything else to happen or people calling.

But they did.

Doc Krinberg

Chapter 20

My uncle called me before I could walk out the door and sadly I had to cut him off, as I would've missed my streetcar downtown. I promised to call home when I could. In the background I could hear my aunt wailing and Nick's voice trying to soothe her.

A grim tableau all around.

The whole ride to my stop on Market Street I couldn't think of anything but Jack. I kept trying to envision what he was doing, what he was suffering, or if the lawyer had buffed him up and cut him a husk. Honestly, I was fearful of him being clipped there or ordered clipped and that word would come locally. As I sat in the window seat I just kept trying to concoct a dialogue to confront the Disney Boys in regards to trusting Jack, not acting hasty. Those guys didn't even trust each other if they were sitting in the same pews in church. I definitely had to make some calls, first and foremost to Francois. I had to get the background on the drop. Then I had to measure the anger and bitterness with the D-boys. I'd decided to use all my bogus phone cards and call Clovis from a pay phone to get a story from him as well.

In all this I forgot I was meeting Sylvia for late lunch at Original Joe's. I walked past the turntable on Powell Street and let the tourists push the car around back into the direction up Powell and I would wait up the street, beating the crush. A guy outside the 49er bar told me I looked like

Tyrone Power, but he was dead. Then another toothless guy who asked me the directions to the Langley Porter Day Room as he was lost, mouth open like McMurphy post lobotomy. It was a typical morning. But 'Manchurian Candidate' was playing at Powell Cinema so I made a mental note to take Sylvia. I gave McMurphy a cigarette and another freak that looked like Tor Johnson after freebasing rock for a year got one too. Morning at Hallidie Plaza.

Dominic was there for an hour, working his jaw and constantly looking at his watch. I knew he had a hair up his ass for some reason, but my dance card of pathos was pretty full. Finally he turned to me.

"Remy." He was looking at the door as he talked, not at me. "That east coast prick you took down south before?"

"Yes, what about him?"

"He say anything about deliveries…being different?"

"Nooo…he really didn't say anything except how he hated 'fruits' and coming to the city. Why?"

"No reason. Fuck him. *He's* probably a fruit. Tough guy!" He spat out. His jaw was crazy and it was driving me nuts as well. Any more of this and he could join the boys on lower Powell.

Once he was gone, I sighed in relief and went out of the office telling the crew to remember to thank any and all customers, especially the pricks, for parking at the Pan-American. I called my dad to get a lay of the land in LA and though Jack's folks were in the basket-weaving sector, he asked me at least five more times if I knew anything about Jack's trip, then cursing Jack out in Greek as my mom wailed in the background 'how could he do this?' I guess our folks didn't know us at all. I must've said more 'I dunno's' to my dad, then lied and said business called. I was waiting for Francois to call, having left a vague hello message on his machine that I knew he monitored. I felt bad cutting my uncle off but I blew off calling him back. Feeling a bit desperate, I called Francois again and invited him up to the City to buy him dinner. If he was shaking down Calloway, I know he knew my work number.

During our lunch rush I usually allowed the boys to stagger their eating times and I walked to Taylor Street and down the hill to meet Sylvia. She had an appointment with an eye doctor whose office was near Chinatown in California Street but she dug eating at Joe's. I swear, sometimes I think she was whiter than me.

"You're not white, Remy. You're Mediterranean. Like Italians, Jews, Arabs."

"What?"

"Seriously, no one is handing you, in your olive skin and shiny black hair any keys to the country club, honey, in this lifetime." She smirked.

"Hmm, I see, and this is from the woman with the Led Zeppelin cassette in her bedroom stereo system?"

"Preference, child, like you and the delta blues. Preference."

And she was right.

So I walked down to Joe's and entering found it was a madhouse. It was as if my entire menu for the day was bedlam; Jack, my family, work, now Joe's. I tried peering around to see her in the sea of lunch goers and tuxedoed waiters skating around with orders or writing down things they forgot. It was too crowded to walk around and as there were quite a few people waiting to get seated I went to the register and asked if there was a single ebony lady seated alone. The look I got was priceless and the head cocked to an area behind the entryway down to the kitchen let me know.

"Thank God you found me. This is a crazy day here for some weird reason." She looked absolutely fine and I told her.

Finally a guy who looked like Fred Gwynne came over and not taking the menu ordered two specials and Miller High Life's. I noticed a couple of people who had stopped eating and were looking at us.

"Does it bother you when people stare at us? I asked.

"Yes and no. When I see hate, yes. When I see envy, no." She smiled. "Hey, I'm in front of you, don't worry about other people."

I thought about that. I could remember quite a few eyes on our first date at the Cantata who looked like they would trade places. Younger guys. The older ones weren't ever happy. And women. I had seen a few hateful looks. For fuck's sake, it was 1978!

"I don't really care when we're together." I was wondering if I should share my bad news.

"So how's life at the Pan-American?" She moved her jaw like she was chewing a brick and I laughed having told her about Dominic.

"So sexy, you wouldn't believe it. Dominic is just about gone so you're looking at the new storage garage union kingpin here. Substantial pay raise too. Yessiree." I raised my eyebrows.

"Oh? How much?"

"A buck-three-eighty." I laughed.

"Asshole!"

And then we ate and I felt her shoeless foot on my ankle, pushing up my pants and playing with my leg. I just stared at her clear, cocoa colored skin, the soft of her face and definition of her jawline; statuesque neck disappearing into a royal blue collared shirt and her charcoal blazer.

Changing my tone, "I might have to jump down to L.A. in the near future, or maybe further south," I tried to sound casual. Fail.

"Okay, to see your mom and dad? Old girlfriends?" She smiled but I could hear curiosity in her voice.

"Yes, my old girlfriends…like Natalie Orloff, or Connie Nefussi. Natalie couldn't decide whether she wanted to look like Francoise Hardy or Brian Jones and stopped talking to me when I went to the marines and became a 'baby killer.' Connie said I wasn't Greek enough and she couldn't stand in a church and be married to such a religious slacker. Sex in her dad's enormous '56 Oldsmobile was okay, but damn, those other rules are sure important. I haven't attended since being confirmed at eight. Yea, guess I'll take care of those two while there…but I had better tell their husbands to move aside." She dipped a finger in her beer and flicked it at me.

"Baby killer! Dater of blondes! Francois Hardy?"

And then I just told her. " My cousin Jack, that you met, is in jail in Panama for cocaine smuggling."

She just stared at me and blinked.

"That's pretty heavy, Remy. Did you know what he was doing?"

"Damn, did my dad tell you to ask that? He's asked me that a hundred times already. No, I didn't. But, he's in trouble and instead of his parents dealing with Panama, I may have to visit him."

"Your cousin didn't seem like the type. He had that 'I drive a hot car so please fuck me now, as I'm busy' type of vibe—and very self centered—but not a drug trafficker. Damn, they just busted a doctor at St. Mary's for pilfering meds, opiates; Tylox, Percodan. Crazy. His whole career destroyed. Poor family."

"Yes." I felt that lameness you get when a lie just doesn't fill in all the gaps for your guilt. I thought of Jack's family, my family.

So we left and I walked her up the hill to California, no minor task after filling up at Joe's. I felt like dying while she kept up a brisk pace.

"C'mon, old white man, don't you know we have an extra muscle in our legs according to grand legend?" That grabbed me. My dad would say that very thing when we watched the Giants play the Dodgers, and he'd comment on Mays's speed in the outfield!

"Okay, but just wait until I get my Eugenics charts…there'll be hell to pay." I was definitely feeling the strain of the walk uphill. At the top, where I exaggeratedly huffed and puffed for her benefit she turned and kissed me and then started to run as the California car was just starting to slide on the tracks. As she alighted onto the outside seats, swinging on the white vertical rail, and hanging sideways I watched her lips moving.

"I love you." She mouthed.

No woman had ever told me that, besides my mother. I watched the car roll away.

Chapter 21

After work, and handing it off to Calloway, looking into his face and his receding hairline to get a clue as to his private vice, I just couldn't see it. He was like an older Lumpy Rutherford. Before I left the phone in the office rang, and I lurched to it ahead of Calloway.

"I got your message, brah. Meet me at dis place," and he rattled off some North Beach address.

"Why are we meeting at a residence?" I was wary of this.

"It's a new house I'm setting up and need to fall by and check onna few tings. Can handle?"

"Can handle." I'd have to.

So, Francois was expanding, and into Italian North Beach. That took balls. I wonder if he had Asian and Polynesian girls there as well. I also wanted to know whom he was in bed with to set up in Little Italy. I always felt they allowed him his book making because of his clientele and the chicken feed it was compared to other bookmakers they owned.

The house was tucked away off Broadway in a corner of North Beach on Castle. I had walked down to Grant and went to Chinatown thru there. I always liked checking out the stores and restaurants, the butcher shops and bars. I stopped at the Buddha Bar and had a shot before making it to Francois' 'new' place. Hopefully I would get a feel for what was up with all the stakeholders and if he had any new intel on Jack. Afterwards I planned on going by City Lights and buying Sylvia a new book to read when in her down time working nights, then a drink at the Vesuvius.

As I approached the house, right on the corner of Green and Castle, I could see a guy sitting in the window blinds drawn just so he was visible by the soft light behind him. He watched me as I walked up the steps. I rang the bell and a small peephole opened and a quiet, island accented voice asked if I was Remy.

"I am."

"What's Twenty-one Area?"

I smiled, "Amphibs and a good shore break." It was the beach area at Camp Pendleton. The door opened.

"Sorry, he make me ask." The guy said.

Like his other places I could smell the kitchen first. He always had something on the stove to make it feel like a home and to not put people off. He'd been in houses all over Asia that had massive infusions of GI's and high turnover rates in service and customers and the smell of the women and whatever cleaning stuff and insecticides made him sick. His girls took turns cooking and they liked hanging out in the kitchen playing cards or watching the small TV in there when not busy. I always felt like I was walking into his personal house when I used to fall by and see Lorna. He wanted his places to look like a normal business, and this house, on a cramped dead end street didn't make sense.

The guy who let me in also looked pure island, like he played linebacker at Kahuku and not getting that scholarship to UH or BYU, fell in with 'uncle' Francois.

"Is he here?" I asked.

"Yea, I get him. Sit down da kitchen, thru der." He pointed at a beaded curtain in an arched doorway. So I went in and there were two girls at the table eating what looked like pancet. They looked up bored, and then went back to eating. I leaned up against the sink and then Francois came in. He was wearing an ancient aloha shirt that had to be stolen from Arthur Godfrey, jeans and huaraches. He lifted his chin, tilted his head and I got up and followed him. I noticed the two girls sit up straighter when he came in as if he were the headmaster entering the classroom. We went up some stairs and down a passageway, past three sets of doors and into a small room that overlooked the backyard that was covered for privacy. There was a guy who looked like the twin of *da kine* I met downstairs. Francois told him to go smoke, and saying nothing he left. After the guy went down the hallway he peeked out after him and then turned to me.

"Dis place gonna make all sorts of cash, and I know you prolly got a hundred questions about how and why but cannot go there now, 'kay?"

"'Okay." He was right.

"So dis is where we at, Jack got dropped in Panama City. From first report dey were on his back like a short overcoat, like dey knew. He was using a new stash; big ass boombox. Had four plus keys inside it. Da Weasel had come thru wit a placebo a month earlier and no problems. Jack, not so much. So, he inna holding area, in general stir, but moving him, if not already, to Carcel Modelo. Dey segregate da locals from Europeans and Americans. Dey also got some Army guys who got popped, but still in military so da base take care of dem. He got a lawyer and from what I hear getting a stake for street connection making his food when at da Modelo. But dats it. His family gonna have to pongo up for his case, his food and goodies real soon, so maybe you go down der and set him straight on all counts."

He paused and made a sour expression on his face, "Da D-Boys not happy and other people involved in this one too. No one is happy and dey sweating it dat Jack may roll—cop a plea and get help from State or DEA. Can happen, eh?"

And that was it.

"You think he hold his mud, or sing?"

I looked out the window. My mouth was dry and after hearing Francois' report my head also hurt. "I think he'll take it standing up. He didn't go in with his eyes shut and he can be tough. He knows its not a life sentence and will take time and money. I also think the powers that be want him to stay happy and they'd give a jolt of cash upfront, a strong jolt of that insurance money I know they have, and send the message of 'hey, we're family, we're here…don't fuck up' if you know what I mean. I want to talk to the Boys, or whoever has the power on this, okay?"

"He's not you Remy, you're da Corps, jungle tough. Jack, he sells fuckin' sports cars. Don't know how big da jolt was but he gonna be taken care of…in da beginning."

"Everybody finds out what they're made of when the shit hits. This is his time." But I sounded like a weak liar. "So tell me, is this all from the Weasel?"

He smiled, "When da Weasel went dark, Corky get spooked and he put eyes in Panama watching Jack deplane and then seeing him taken off by uniform guys. Da Weasel was about 15' behind Jack, lighting a cigarette when it happen So dats where I hear it from. Corky and da others. Yo cuz Clovis took a huge hit on dis, Elihu too. They have people waitin' up and down *da kine*"

"Elihu tried to bail, did you know that?"

"No, how you know?"

"When the Weasel went dark, he called me and I went to his house. He asked me if I wanted to buy in, take his stake, as he was afraid. Mona told me as much too. I said no and left."

He had a faraway look in his eye, almost dreamy. He spoke softly, "You going to have to go down der and square him away, and soon. Also get his folks in line for pay-offs. He on his own. Remember what dey told you on your ride, eh?"

"Yea, I do." It was all champagne and roses if you made it home but if they caught you it was FUBYOYO-fuck you buddy you're on your own.

"Wanna blow job while you're here? I gotta little Viet girl if you wanna time trip." He laughed. I didn't like his laugh.

I shook my head no, "Its okay. I need to get home." Then I remembered, and while I might be skating on thin ice, I had to deal with it, " What gives with my night manager at the Pan-American?"

He laughed hard, "Shit Remy, you shoulda been a private dick. Calloway? He a degenerate gambler. He pretty much spent his kids' college tuitions betting on fucking everything, even da money he made off you in da Oak-Denver game spent, gone inna New Yawk second."

"Hey, I need him. Please don't take any more bets for him. I need that asshole. I'm taking over there as manager, okay?" I tried to insert both humor and pleading in my voice. A giant hand fell on my shoulder softly, like a tarantula.

"I cut him loose. He all paid off right now, no vig, no nothing. He did drop a lot of jeedas on da Ali-Spinks fight. Who would've thought, eh?"

"Semper fi."

"Semper fi, braddah."

City Lights was on the way to Vesuvio's and I definitely needed a bracer after hearing that sad newsbreak. I went inside and wanted to go downstairs to get out of the crowd and tourists and look for something she'd enjoy.

I came around the corner of one stack and there stood Mona. What struck me was that I'd never seen her in public, alone or away from Elihu, so taking a step back I just watched her. There was a space around her that people just gave away, not crowding her or being too close. She had a shoulder bag of some extinct reptile and covering her torso was a black serape. And I had never seen her wearing glasses either. I couldn't see what she was reading, but she was in the philosophy and sociology area. I backed up and just walked out and went straight to Vesuvio's for a drink. I needed it. I planned on calling Nick when I got home explaining a few things he would need to know, and tell him to be cool or my uncle would be all up in my shit. I called Sylvia from the bar too.

"Sounds like you're having fun. Listen, I'm starting nights for two weeks day after tomorrow so you had better give it up before that."

"I'm in North Beach had to see a buddy. Two days? Okay, tomorrow night, pack a toothbrush and a LBD."

"Damn, take charge."

I laughed, "Call you tomorrow."

I ordered one more drink, felt a little more human and decided on splurging on a taxi. I also reflected on seeing Mona 'in the wild.' That was just sort of weird. On the ride home I revisited my conversation with Francois and I also had a lot of thoughts going thru my head about Mr. Berberian and why he disappeared.

Chapter 22

My conversation with Nick wasn't very good. His telling of the effect on his parents from Jack's bust was in a word, catastrophic. They were in a state of shock and humiliation. Nick laid it out:

"I'm going down there next week, Monday. I have to meet this guy Marainos who claims to be his lawyer, as per the state department and see what's needed."

"Have they moved him to the prison facility yet?" I asked, hoping that they did.

"Yea, he's in a place…" I could hear him going thru some papers, "…a place called Carcel Modelo. They've segregated him. They keep all the non-latinos in a different area. Is that a good thing?" I could hear the strain in his voice.

"That's good Nick, listen, if you're leaving Monday I want to come to LA on Saturday and meet. I want to tell you a few things to relate to Jack, need to say. Its super important and it has to do with his safety, okay? I don't want to go into it too deep but I know some of the people he went down there for. This is between you and I. It goes nowhere else. Do not tell your folks. We really need to meet and if you weren't making this trip so quickly, I would be going, okay? I'm not bullshitting here. This is important and especially for Jack maintaining down there." I sounded urgent because I was.

"You knew all about it didn't you Remy? You knew he was going. Why in the fuck didn't you stop him?" He didn't sound angry, just tired.

"Nick, this is Jack we're talking about. Have you ever stopped him from doing what he wanted?"

"No, not me, but maybe you could've. So what do I tell my folks in the meantime and what else should I prepare before I go?" The change I had front-loaded the phone with fell, time to feed it again. "Are you in a phone booth?"

"Yea, hey, how much money did this lawyer say to bring? What's his name again?"

"Marainos. He said he needed five-k right now. I have five-k like I have blonde hair."

"You're going to bring seven thousand five hundred dollars. I'll take care of that part—the five thou—and kick in the two thousand five hundred, just do not tell your folks. He's going to start adding things on and you need to be prepared. You're not just paying him, you're paying a whole network of people he's going to have on hand to help Jack, from extra shit paper to protection from rape, if need be. Look, let's talk on Saturday when I get there. I have the weekend off, my girl is working nights, so carve some time out for me, alright?"

He sighed, and I hoped I had helped lift a little weight off of him, "Yea, alright. Remy, who are these guys he's in with? They're all bad actors aren't they?" He said it rhetorically, he knew what they were about. "Girlfriend? You? I thought you had turned into a zen monk after Viet-Nam."

"Even monks need to rock'n'roll, man. I'll see you Saturday. Tell your folks to also keep in mind; Jack has a flat up here. Whatever they want to do with it, sublet, release, I can take care of that entire deal here with a POA, get that from Marainos, okay? We'll talk on Saturday." I didn't want to push ten pounds of shit into Nick's five-pound bag anymore than I had to.

"Thanks. Hey…"

"What?"

"He's in a lot of danger, isn't he?"

"Yes he is. I won't lie. Its why we need to have to do a few things while he's there."

And that was it. I was a little relieved after talking to Nick, the sanest of the three of us. I called Elihu and told him we needed to talk ASAP. He said okay, drop by now. I also called Francois and left a message with whoever he had at this number that 'the weather down south would be much cooler come next week and to stop sweating it'.

I had maintained my bike at Hugo so it was very late when I rolled up on Elihu's Filbert house. I felt like I hadn't slept in a week I was so fatigued from the bust. I had only gotten the news today and it already felt like a month of Mondays. Mona answered the door in a see thru negligee, a cigarette in a long, sleek ebony holder.

"He's in the parlor as usual." She motioned behind her with the holder. I tried not to look, failed. Before I walked down the passageway I looked at the stand in the entryway that obviously they threw their mail on and saw a book on it. I sort of drifted up to it and saw it was Sartre's 'Being and Nothingness.' I strolled down the hall to his lair He looked like utter fuck. His hair had this Einstein thing going on and I could see the ashtray was stuffed and over flowing with his Gauloises. Mona smoked Virginia Slims and I didn't see any of hers. His eyes were bloodshot and his little china bowl was half filled with blow and a few rolled up twenties in various states of operation. I sat down across from him after I turned the TV off.

"Eli, how long did you know that Jack had dropped?"

"Four days ago." He reached over for a fresh cigarette. I explained my conversation with Nick and my upcoming trip to LA. He smoked quietly as I related the conversation, just nodding his head.

"What I need from you, and if others wish to contribute, are any specific things you wish to impart to Jack or his lawyer, that has his brother's confidence. Can you do that?" He wasn't catatonic but he looked like he was in the deep and narrow tunnel too much blow can put you in; accompanied by the 60 fathom stare.

"I'm sorry I didn't call you. Looking back, we should've called you when we found out. This was a bad deal all around." He had started rerolling a $20 as he talked and when it was tight enough leaned in and took a blast straight from the bowl. He tilted his head back and running his fingers over his nostrils sniffed a few times and then shook as if he had a violent chill. I sensed something and looked to see Mona standing in the doorway, one finger pointed at her ear doing circles to imply he was nuts.

"Elihu, you need to stop. Remy, tell him to stop. He hasn't since he heard about Jack. No shower, no fucking, no nothing." She said with disgust.

"Eli…Eli? Look at me," I said as he turned his head slowly I could see his pinned pupils, almost invisible in his pale, china blue eyes. "Make sure you get whatever marching orders for me before I leave for LA Saturday morning, alright?"

He nodded, picked up the TV remote and back on it went. Carol Doda appeared on the Perfect 36 from San Jose, and I turned away. I wondered if she and Mona danced together at the Condor. Mona asked me if I wanted a beer and I felt like I needed one so I followed her out of the parlor, through the old space that was a butler's pantry into the kitchen. Mercifully, only the light over the sink was on because I didn't need to be staring at her in a bright light as it was bad enough when she opened the refer to get a bottle and back lit almost nude.

"He's spooking me big time. He's on the verge of pyschosis. When it happened, that fucking guy Spin came by and got all up in his grill over Jack. Elihu then brought up the first guy, the D-Boys's friend who Od'd. Then Spin grabbed him by the shirtfront. Scared him." She looked over at the doorway and then whispered, "Who is Justin? Spin said if things were bad, and Jack was singing, Justin would fly south again."

Justin. I had only heard of him during one of Francois' lapses of discretion. He was a cleaner they used on special occasions. Fucking oath, they must really be sweating this one hard. I hoped my message to François had cooled some tempers. I asked Mona if they *were* going to fly him south, if Spin had said that.

"No…not yet. They said wait until his family gets involved and the skids get greased for the lawyer. Anyway, before Jack was in a facility that's like a big pig pen but now is in the real jail." The refer door was still open, and her nipples were rock hard. I kept trying to get a grip.

"Okay, well, hopefully things will stabilize." I finished my beer in a long swallow, and felt as if I could sleep standing up. "Fuck, I am beat. Thanks for the beer, I'm off, like shorts in the night."

"You look dead Remy. We have extra rooms. Stay here and just get up early." She walked out of the kitchen and I could hear her talking to Eli. She came back in. "Take the guest room at top of the landing. I'll bring extra towels and you have your own *benjo* too. Come on, Elihu thinks it's a good idea as well. He'll see you early, have some coffee and maybe he'll get normal again, 'k?"

I didn't relish the ride home and I was dead on my feet. I just nodded and followed. I kept my eyes down going up the stairs.

I had never been up there before and was amazed at how opulently appointed the guest room was. I thought I had gone back to pre-earthquake days. Whatever weirdness Elihu possessed he certainly had an eye for restoration, canopy beds, antiques and all. The bed was so high there was a step stool on the side to mount it when I was undressed. I had folded all my clothes and after washing, I climbed up on this big ass bed and feeling like the 1890's I fell dead asleep.

I had one of those panic—shit your pants moments; you wake up in a place and you're immediately filled with dread. Then I remembered I was in Elihu's Victorian bedroom. There was a sliver of moonlight piercing the drapes where they were parted and it threw a band across the floor and up onto the lower part of the bed. I pulled myself up and sat with my back against the brass bars of the head. I needed a cigarette, so I leaned over and pulled the lanyard on the small nickel-plated lamp. The shade on this was an ornate stained glass affair with different sections that diffused the light nicely for bedroom dark pupils. By comparison, my nightstand lamp was like a klieg. I snatched up my cigarettes and lighter and turned towards the dark side of the room and almost shit myself again. Mona was sitting in the high backed wooden chair next to the armoire.

"Fuck! What the hell, Mona?"

She put her finger to her lips to make me quiet and noiselessly glided to the bed. She still had her see thru bedclothes on.

"Elihu is still awake downstairs, but he isn't normal. He's amped out and buzzing like a bee. He's in like a trance he's done so much blow. I hate that shit. He likes rubbing it on my pussy but then I cant feel a thing down there."

"Ohhhkay…and so why are we talking? What time is it?" The whole scene was bizarre.

"I need you to know something. They want to snuff out Jack. Elihu doesn't really think he can handle and will roll. They're going to wait until his brother talks to him, with all your messages and info and then give him a little bit of light after that. But if the lawyer gives them a signal he's going south, they'll snuff him out. I know he's your blood." I just sat there finally lighting my cigarette, listening to her. "Another thing, Remy, they're not sure about the Weasel. They think perhaps he may have sold Jack out and Elihu's scared because of the way he acted when the Weasel disappeared—its casting suspicion. For all we know he's still down south. This lawyer may be working for Jack, but he's also working for *them*, so know that before you talk to Jack's brother. *Wakaramasuka?*"

"*Wakarimasen.*" Yea, I understood too well.

She smiled in the semi dark, "Now you owe me."

"Thanks, Mona. I truly appreciate this." And I did. It just reaffirmed things I had been thinking.

"So show me some appreciation." Her hand was under the blanket and I felt her strong fingers find me, close around me. She leaned in and kissed me. And stayed. I felt myself responding and had to pull back.

"Mona, you know I'm involved, okay?" I tried to plead. This was the last thing I needed.

"I don't care Remy." She pouted. "I liked that. A good kiss lasts years after it actually occurs."

"Because you're with Elihu, and I feel this tension between you and me. And what about Elihu?" I raised an eyebrow.

"He's catatonic, and anyway he's been limp for weeks. Hmm, I see you have no such worries," she smiled, "Just fuck me Remy, I need it." She wasn't pleading, and said it matter of factly. "I saw you at City Lights. Why didn't you say hello?"

I didn't know why and told her so.

"Did you feel weird seeing me in public and not here or somewhere with Elihu?"

"I did," I said honestly. "I didn't wish to bother you. I don't like it when I'm absorbed in a book and people hassle me."

"I wouldn't have minded. Do you read?"

"I do…but not Sartre." She raised an eyebrow. "I like Maugham. And Nietzsche. Henry Miller."

"I like Miller too. *The Air Conditioned Nightmare* is one of my favorites."

I couldn't believe we were having this conversation with my erection in her hand! Being beleaguered wasn't going to stand up in this court, so I just got out of bed not knowing what time it was, kissed her on top of her head as if she were a niece, got dressed and froze my ass off going home.

All I could think about was the memory of Sylvia mouthing those words as the cable car jerked away.

Chapter 23

Needless to say I was a fuckstory the next day. I packed a small douche kit & ditty bag for later, called the hotel to ensure my reservation on a king bed. San Francisco isn't so popular in early spring so rooms are available. I made a flight reservation on PSA as Delta morning flights were booked solid and I'd be in LA Saturday morning. When I rolled into work I stashed my bike and then I was surprised to find a guy in a very sharp suit, alone in the office, obviously waiting for me.

"Hello." I said nonchalantly, putting my gear away. "Can I help you, sir?" I had no idea who he was; disgruntled customer, a Fed or one of Dom's buddies.

"Remy, right?" He said standing up, extending a hand.

"Yes," and as I shook his hand, "and you are…?"

Still smiling, still cheerful, "I'm an old friend of Dominic's. I wanted to drop by and meet you. You know, face to face, ask a question or two." He sat down, straightening his tie. I was attracted to one of his eyes as it never moved, the pupil was fixed and he moved his head a bit to the other side so the real eye could take me in. The other was glass.

"Like?" I didn't know who this ginzo was and already regretting his appearance at the garage.

He smiled blandly, pulled a pack of Pall Malls from his inner jacket pocket. "May I smoke?" I gestured with an upturned palm, and moved an ashtray closer in to where he was sitting. "Just a few things. First of all, how's the transition, you taking the helm, as it were?" He tilted his head back, blew smoke at the ceiling, and I saw the light glimmer off his bogus eye.

"Smooth," I smiled, "No worries. Dominic did a good job handing it off. Was there something you really wanted to know, Mr...?"

"I'm so sorry. Matranga, Phil Matranga." He held out his hand again, we repeated all formalities a second time and he pulled a card from the same pocket he took his cigarettes from. "How rude of me."

My patience was dead, but I also knew cordiality was on the menu for this guy, and respect goes a long way in his world, if anything out of my own for Dominic.

He smiled again," I can see you're a guy who wants to get at the heart of things, am I right? So first off, congrats on taking the managerial position as it saved us some heartache. The owner is very satisfied with the choice and the other issue is this: When we tell you to shit, you ask how much and what color. When we tell you to vote and who to vote for you become a good little marine again and say 'aye aye, sir' and when we ask any other favors please follow them to the letter. Now you deal directly with us, specifically me. Understand?" His voice hadn't lost its new morning cheeriness and he had smiled throughout. I nodded my head in affirmation. He was a Disney Boy in an expensive suit.

Again his charm swept the room, "Great!" He pulled another card from his coat pocket.

I stared at it, "A florist?"

"Yes, I recommend these guys. Quick, efficient and always do great work, and they're down on the peninsula."

"Why?" But I didn't really want to know.

"Your last name is Karras, right? Well there, Mr. Remy Karras,

Dominic was just *skimming* along, minding his own and had an accident." He put out his cigarette, stood and buttoned his suit jacket. "Let's stay in touch, shall we? It was great meeting you." He started for the door, turned ever so slowly, "And…sorry for your loss." Then he just glided right out. I just sat there. I heard the time clock punched as I heard the guys handing out parking tickets or double stamped for people leaving. I heard voices and cars moving.

I was just numb. I reflected on Dominic's behavior, how skittish he'd become in the last few weeks and before the hand over and that random question about whether Mr. Jersey-accent had asked about any deliveries being light. So he'd been skimming. I wondered how much and how long. Then I noticed a new set of green ledger books on the edge of the desk, opening I found them coded to start on this date and the old ones I knew would be gone from the safe. Tony, one of the day guys came into the office very slowly.

"Remy?"

I just looked up and opened my eyes wider in acknowledgement.

"That was so weird about Dominic. Wow. His poor wife finding him in the garage." I tilted my head towards him to continue, "You didn't hear? He passed out or had a heart attack and was in the car with the engine running. Angela found him."

I had a grim inner smile at the sense of humor these guys had; from garage to garage. Dust to dust. Why in the fuck couldn't they just ask for the money back?

"Poor Dom. Who told you guys?"

"That nice guy from corporate. The one who just left? Man, they must own every garage in the City."

"I'm sending flowers. Start a collection." There was nothing else to do.

"Will do." And he went back outside.

What the hell else was going to happen?

At about 3:30, I heard a deep gruff voice outside the office as I sat with the bookkeeper we kept on tap to pinch hit for the regular guy whose nickname was Mr. Peabody for his huge round glasses. But since Peabody didn't show I can only surmise he and Dominic are together somewhere. Then Francois appeared at the doorway. Fuck! I was already depressed at the suit's news concerning Dom and his skimming. The bookkeeper wasn't much help but we did figure out there had been two sets of books, and now this guy was at my door.

"Bonjour, Francois." I said flatly, lighting a cigarette. The dead grey eyes looked at the bookkeeper that nervously said we should pick things up tomorrow.

Francois came in and closed the door.

"I didn't want to use da phone because I'm not sure what lines are clean, eh?"

"Is it like that?" I wondered if my house phone had been tapped yet or would it.

"You been by Jack's flat?"

"No, and I need to fall by there pronto. There are just a few stones in my pathway now…serious business transitions here." I didn't wish to discuss the details with him.

"You may wanna look into his flat ASAP, 'k? A little bird says a warrant for a search could be by Thursday at the latest, so maybe you talk to da landlord prior, eh? Maybe gotta a pic of you and Jack together so he see your family?"

"Don't need it, the landlord knows me. By Thursday?"

"Yea, when you went LA?"

"I'm going Saturday morning, back Saturday night." I gestured to the

Pan-American garage office, "This is my mafia day job."

"Hah!" He barked, "Dats no shit. All downtown covered. Dey got quite a portfolio, eh Remy?"

"Any other word on Jack?" I was still nervous about his status and from Mona's secret confession.

"He's good. So far. You see 'Magnificent Seven'?"

I nodded my head.

"When Steve McQueen and Yul Brynner are rolling da coffin to boot hill on da hearse and Brynner asks McQueen howzit?"

Where was this going?

"And McQueen goes someting like he knew dis guy fell offa one 10 story building, and he pass a window washer on da eighth floor who asks him 'howzit?' and da guy falling say 'so far so good.' Dat's Jack, so far so good. He ain't hit bottom yet" And then he got up and walked out whispering the usual 'semper fi' meaning we were done.

I remembered McQueen in that role as a gunfighter who was tired of the trade and wanted a piece of land and a quiet life. I started to envy his insight.

Doc Krinberg

Chapter 24

"Wake up, Remy, you promised."

I had passed out from pure fatigue; the nightmare of Elihu's, the stress of finding out Dominic had been clipped and the pending warrant for Jack's flat to be tossed by the Feds pulled me down who no doubt were also looking for Jack's KA's and family members who might be in on things and perhaps they were already looking at me. Four keys of Peruvian Dancing Powder tend to grab people's attention. I had promised to take Sylvia to the Hurricane Bar, and so got out of bed and started dressing, enjoying her enjoying watching me.

"So I guess being here means we're doing this thing, it isn't just a fling," she said nonchalantly.

I pulled my coat on and adjusted my collar, "Should I bother with the tie?" I asked her, ignoring her declaration, smiling.

"Yes, leave it off because I want to strangle you with it later and that's easier when not already around your neck."

I chuckled. "Yea, we're doing this. We're not exactly the Loving's, and this adult romance is all new to me, but I like it. I wonder which room my folks were in when they made me here?" Weird thought but it popped into my head.

"Oh, the Loving's? Getting historical on me." She rose out of her seat, came to me and put her hands behind my head, looking up into my eyes. Her voice was very soft, very low.

"I like how you wear a suit, and it doesn't wear you. I like the way you wear me too, how we fit together." Her fingers were curling their way into my hair and then one came down and was unzipping me. "I like how you feel in my hand. How you get so hard for me Remy, just from my fingers brushing you," she pulled me out; I imagined how that looked exposed next to the navy blue of my trousers. She went on, "But before we go to the famous Hurricane Bar, there's something else I'd like." And pulling me by it walked back over to the bed turned her back to me, bending her mini already high on her ass and thighs.

That was probably the last best night of my life.

Chapter 25

I hadn't told Francois I had a key to Jack's as he had given it to me before he left. I didn't want him horning in on my search knowing I could walk right in so I had fibbed about the landlord. The last thing Jack needed was a part of the crew that was already leaning hostile against him ransacking his flat for whatever reason. So far Francois was playing a neutral role but I was taking no chances. I was kicking myself in the ass for not jumping down here after I found he had been dropped and wondered if it had already been tossed or burgled.

I told the boys at work I had a Dr.'s appointment in Pacifica and gave the office keys to Mel, a guy I could trust and told him the new bookkeeper would drop by later. And so out to Noe Valley I flew.

Jack's flat was off Noe and 25th Street. He hated living in the Avenues as they tended to be cooler and foggy and in his valley there he enjoyed more sun, saying it reminded him of a funky Los Angeles. Noe was also going thru a gentrification by yuppies and gay men who like Jack were attracted to it for the beautiful houses and apartment flats. He called my three-story garret on Hugo something out of a Hammett story. He did like the Stein, on 9th and Irving that served room temperature Guinness.

"Other than that place and the Greek deli between 8th and 7th, your neighborhood is about as bland as Clovis' Okie old man." He'd laugh. Jack, always climbing. Always comparing.

I drove thru his neighborhood wearing a full birdcage with the visor down, and did a couple of loops looking at cars and vans, into doorways. Francois had me paranoid and my radar was up. I didn't see any suspicious cars as the Feds usually used unmarked Fords. I parked the bike over near Lick Junior High and hoofed it over to his place.

The steps were bathed in the early spring light and were swept clean. At Jack's entry there were a couple of advertisers, throwaways, and nothing else that said the tenant was gone. Taking one last look over my shoulder I turned the key and went in, pushing a stack of letters, sliding them out in a swath ahead of me. That was a good omen. No front entry. Out of habit I said, 'hello' like an idiot and walked in, leaving my shoes at the door. I never wore shoes into anybody's flat with the exception of Elihu's who the first time I ever came over asked if I were a 'Jap,' even in front of Mona. Now I wanted to be quiet and keep shoe prints off the surface. His flat looked perfectly clean with the exception of a fine layer of dust on the wooden coffee table in his front room that overlooked 25th with bay windows. The room looked intact from what I could tell and the dust on the tabletop correlated with the dust accumulated on a semi black-glossy Playboy on its top. That said plenty. I didn't know of any cops who had the self-control *not* to pick it up and thumb thru it.

The dining room was the same. Clean and tidy with the corresponding dust layer intact, untouched. I went into the rooms in the back to include the kitchen and was glad his drapes were pulled so if anyone were watching from behind they wouldn't see movement. I turned on the light in his bedroom and it just yawned back. Nothing. Except a large manila envelope on the dresser secured with a blob of ceiling wax, the letter J embedded in it. I didn't take Jack for a ceiling wax type of guy, but there it was with my name written on it. I inspected the rest of the room and his closet. His dresser and its drawers turned up nothing but clothes and his accessories. How many cufflinks does a guy need? His nightstand also revealed nothing with the exception of a stash of Trojans, cigarettes and a beat up copy of a Philip K. Dick novel.

I looked at the envelope and went back to the front room and peeking onto the street wondered if there was a telephoto lens on the house the whole time. I could always tell the truth; I'm his closest relative and he asked me to drop by if he hadn't returned and now in jail, it's a family thing. So I calmed myself thinking that; the concerned cousin with a key. I was then tempted to pick up the phone to hear tell tale clicking for a trace, but decided not to. I returned to the privacy of his room, sat on the bed and opened the envelope:

> Remy,
>
> Sadly, if you're reading this I'm obviously not there and am either dead or in the slam. So help me out here: If Dead...
>
> My insurance policy is in the small BR converted into an office next to hall bathroom. Look in top desk drawer. Also in there my entire bank books, checks, etc. There is a six-month advance rent in effect so by the time you see this I'll probably be good for five more. The checkbook dates will tell you how much and how long, and address of the real landlord, (not that fake asshole who thinks he manages it upstairs) and his phone #. Discontinue rent, place furniture in storage and help Nick sort it out. If you need ready cash, key to safety deposit box is taped under drawer of same desk. Its at Hibernia Bank on Market, #8493, your name is with the bank as a co-signer as per my instructions. My car is title free, so give it to Nick, all documentation is under checkbook. Car is in storage at Olympic Garage on Sutter (sorry, but much better rates than

yours!). Please help my folks get thru it. It's a lot to ask but I know you're a conscientious prick. Help yourself to any and all of my clothes. You need an upgrade.

If Arrested:

Don't give my car to Nick! I'm also paid up at the Olympic for 6 months so follow up on that too please? Continue my rent checks past 6 months if need be, if you need to make a withdrawal or switch funds from savings to checking do so. Try and square things with the D-boys and my folks as best as you can. And do whatever you can do to get my release. If you need cash, look into my safe deposit.

Don't tell me how stupid I am. I know all that. But know this…what's one of your favorite old marine sayings? "Fucked up like a soup sandwich?" And how!!

As ever,

Jack

I'm glad he didn't ask a lot! Fucking guy.

Everything was just disjointed and out of kilter for the rest of the day. Things at the Pan-American were running smooth but I was still shook up over the whole deal with Dominic. Processing that horror story was hard. I had pushed it aside because of Jack and my promised night with Sylvia; obligations of the heart I couldn't sidestep but I had to follow up on the flowers and pay my respects to him. He helped me when I needed work and like me had been a bush marine and in his glory, an island raider. I planned on riding down to the Peninsula and visiting the funeral home for the evening showing. The funeral I would skip.

I didn't want to go to Elihu's anymore, or meet Francois at the roadhouse. If we needed to meet it would be in public places where I could see downfield and get a glimpse of any surveillance, unless I absolutely had to. I didn't want to pull any Secret Squirrel or Morocco Mole type of shit, be in a secluded place and all of a sudden have guys there I didn't know for whatever reason unless it was impossible. And no more visits to Sylvia's. Her place was off limits if anyone was tailing me for whatever reason. Eight plus pounds of pure cocaine bought that type of paranoia.

I rode down to the funeral home and walking in slowly, saw the sign with Dom's name and proceeding down the hallway could hear the low level, piped in organ music that was damn creepy. I wondered if Dominic had any of his marine raider buddies visiting or some of the bush guys he was with at Henderson Field on Guadalcanal. He never mentioned if any lived in the Bay Area, but when they had their annual meet and greet at The Marine's Memorial Hotel I could count on him being trashed pretty near all week and running the garage myself.

I pushed into the room and saw two people inside. A woman in a black shawl sitting in the first row and an attendant looking at his watch as if he were ready to button it up. The woman in black had to be Angela. I walked slowly towards the casket and glimpsed over at her as I came abreast. She was asleep. I went to Dominic and looking at his waxen face I made the sign of the cross. The attendant sent a discreet 'pssst' my way. I walked to him quietly.

"Family or friend?"

"Friend."

"She's been asleep for two hours. Could you?"

I said I'd wake her up.

Angela had aged another twenty years in the last couple of days and walking her to the car took awhile. She turned to me at the car door and in a faraway voice, not even looking at me.

"He used to sing to me. Sinatra, Dean Martin, Mel Torme...can you imagine? Him?"

That made me laugh and I told her 'no.'

"Know what else? He saved money like an *ebreo*. I found a note and inside the mattress was a ton of money! I haven't even counted it all. In the note he said move to Florida. Can you imagine that?"

Riding home I kept thinking of him. How his jaw must've been moving when they came to visit him that last time. Then I thought of Jack; one dead, one in jail. Not a good place.

I remember smoking like a chimney on that hour flight to LA, rehearsing a few things in my head about what Nick needed to say to the lawyer in Panama City. I would also tell him do not talk to any federal guys besides State. No DEA or other such entities as they would spin him and make threats. Just get to the lawyer, and then set Jack on his path. Find out the costs of food, clothes, things to trade, etc. Carry any and all private messages back just to me and try and leave their parents out of the loop on that score as much as possible.

I also had $7500 in cash for him to give immediate relief and to hold the lawyer in his place. Marainos wanted $5000 up front, and that part came from Jack's safe deposit box. The five was to grease Marainos, show him we were in good faith and to start spending it on the wheels of justice. The $2500 was for Jack's personal expenditures to his street connections and giving him an account the lawyer could hold and Jack could draw on. That money goes a long way in a country like that. I hadn't told anyone I was coming down with the exception of Clovis and we would meet privately and have a nice talk concerning Jack, and our northern Californian friends. I didn't wish to deal with my uncle and aunt and my dad had gone off the deep end calling me to rant about Jimmy Carter selling the fucking canal and that Trujillo had made a deal to catch all smugglers before they hit the US with their cocaine and heroin. So it was Jimmy Carter's fault now. I decided to sidestep this weirdness.

I remembered when Jack and I were busted for stealing bikes during our young and wild thief days; two sweet Raleigh's that were locked together at Roxbury Park. We always figured if we stole from some kid in Beverly Hills, they could probably buy another. We didn't count on another set of thieves blowing the whistle on us, and being hauled away by the cops. We'd crossed a turf line and paid for it. Two very pissed off dads came to pick us up at the BHPD. Suspicion of theft! You would've thought we had murdered the Black Dahlia.

So the whole ride home we got the silent treatment as the two of them stewed and burned in the front seat, building up a head of steam. We sat there trying not to laugh and just waiting for them to put us on full blast and they didn't let us down. We hit a red light on Olympic Blvd. and it started. We heard the ashamed mothers speech, the criminal path, amoral living, behaving like Negroes…oh yea, even that. We suffered a couple of weeks of being grounded, various chores and fixing things in the yard, etc. The cops dropped the charges, eventually.

Then we lay in wait at Roxbury with lead pipes and catching one of the Roxbury gang beat the piss out of him. The bike he was loading into a pickup, well, we just borrowed it. We weren't even in high school yet. We'd rode all the way back to our neighborhood, me peddling, Jack atop the handlebars giving directions, and we'd laughed our asses off. Not so funny now. Not a joke to share with Sylvia.

Nick was a basket case when we met and I discussed my end of it, some dictated directly by the D-Boys.

"Remy, I really thought he had something solid going on there selling cars. He was so good at it. He's killing our folks. Where in the hell are they going to raise any money for that shyster down south? I know they borrowed on the mortgage to help me in school." He spoke like a dream walker, the disembodied and not even close to consciousness. That this could happen to his brother was beyond him. Though different and somewhat estranged they were pulled close by Nick's adoration for him. He shook his head slowly.

"You know, I just got engaged. Yes, like a day before we got the news. Can you imagine my telling her this? What her family would think? I was going to surprise my folks and hers but I told her my mom isn't well so lets put it off a bit. I'm already lying to her Remy. I'm turning into Jack!" I let him go on until he ran out of gas. Then again I started the rundown on the info he had to carry to Jack and the money for the lawyer. Seeing the cash, he felt relieved, as his parents had given him $500 for the lawyer. A dope lawyer. Five hundred dollars. He would've thrown Nick out of his office. We went over it again.

"How do you know all this shit? You were in on it." I shook my head no.

"No, in all honesty, I had nothing to do with this run. Don't ask me anything else." I wasn't ready to play true confessions. Then out of nowhere:

"Did you know the French just had a huge nuclear test in the Pacific?"

"I didn't know that. Maybe they'll mutate some giant crabs," I laughed.

"Yea, like that movie where they ate people's heads and talked liked them. You slept over one time and we all stayed up and watched it. A Friday. Then we had cereal for breakfast and we all watched Johnny Quest." He shook his head. "Fuck. This is fucked."

I agreed. Very much so. He dropped his head and shook it slowly from side to side.

"Engaged, Remy. I'm there." He sounded pathetic and it just made me miss Sylvia. "Have you ever been in love?"

I am in love. But I didn't say it, "C'mon, man, I'm a crazed vet waiting to take out a post office or a Thrifty's, I have no time for that love bullshit." I said in mock seriousness.

"I'll try to laugh, but just out of respect and family, okay?" He smiled.

"Please Nick, just tell him to be cool, and you be firm with the lawyer." I must've repeated everything a zillion times, and then I looked at my watch; Clovis, in forty-five minutes up on Sunset at Ben Frank's.

"Thanks Remy. Thanks for the money. I'm so worried about Jack." Then I remembered something.

I described the Weasel, and even wrote out his description and told Nick, "Don't ask why let me know okay? If you can let me know from the hotel, that's great." Poor guy. I had flattened his brain.

"What's her name?"

"Sofia." He smiled.

We bullshitted a little bit more about mindless stuff we did as kids even singing the Tom Slick and Super Chicken theme song and he told me more about Ms. Sofia Andropos, a real Greek girl to make his mom happy. We finally shook hands and then said goodbye. As I walked away he thanked me and without turning I held up a peace sign.

Chapter 26

I went to the nondescript rental car I picked out and drove out Robertson and then up San Vicente to the Strip. The Strip was Clovis' turf. I couldn't stand it, as it screamed 'take-off artists' and that's pretty much what Clovis was. He'd take you off for anything or anyone. And Ben Franks was as phony a rendezvous as you could get. Back in the day when Clovis was fresh from Francois' crime school he was hanging out at Ben Franks, selling dope, and said one of the guys from Hollywood Squares started hitting on him. Clovis was convinced everyone in Hollywood was a 'homo'. It was one of his 'Clovisisms;' the world according to him. I prayed Meredith wouldn't be with him, as I didn't care too much for her company. She flogged the 'I'm British' act a little too hard and would always, in whatever the conversation, tell you it was so much better in England. Once Jack, fed up with her high falutin' ways smiled, pointed at his teeth said loudly 'Are these better in England?' She piped down accordingly after that. Jack was mildly fixated on her just for the fact she was British, but wouldn't admit it for anyone.

I parked and waited a second to see if anyone followed me in but the parking lot had only five cars in it, one the MG that belonged to my older and nefarious cousin. I went inside and walked by the booth he sat in that overlooked the parking lot and went to the men's room. I looked at the walls thoroughly, then took a leak, walked and went to his table. I sat and faced him. As he swirled a spoon in a cream filled coffee he smiled.

"Hah! You remembered." Years ago when Jack and I used to deal small quantities of grass for him while in high school we had a system for meet ups. If Clovis felt like he was under surveillance, and at times he was, we would meet at Franks or some other place in West LA and he would leave a small X made of wet toilet paper on the wall somewhere low, so only if you were really looking for it could see. A few times we'd have to wait until a guy was done shitting to check it out.

No X today.

"Yea, who could forget all your Dick Tracey crime stopper shit?"

Clovis loved Dick Tracy and knew probably every villain from Coffee Head to 88 Keys.

I ordered a grilled cheese and coffee when the waitress sidled up to give Clovis a refill.

"Okay, so let me know what's up?"

I related my discussion with Nick, the only omission being that if he saw the Weasel to contact me. I also told him money would be a problem with our aunt and uncle and since he was family, Clovis needed to pongo up with some cash. I could see by his eyes that that wasn't such a hot idea for him. He flutter-blinked and made a clucking sound when shit hit him the wrong way. He had done it since I met him in the early 1950's when I was a little kid.

"Do you have confidence Jack won't try and roll and help the DEA?" He asked leaning over.

"I do. I think he'll stand and take it, do whatever time they give him, or we can buy for him. Are the people from the North amiable to chip in another jolt, or no?"

He shook his head. "They're very pissed off, very paranoid. You know the Weasel still hasn't come home and his non availability prior to this clambake raised eyebrows." He took a second to pan the parking lot and then got up and walked to the cigarette machine near the door to get some matches from the bowl on top.

I knew he was looking out at Sunset Blvd. If anyone could spot metro, vice or narcotics division guys it was Clovis. He came back to the table.

"There is a belief that the Weasel sold Jack, for whatever reason. They don't know if he was squeezed and made a deal to give him up for what was behind Door #1 or if he's with some other cartel that's hitting the pipelines of *our* cartel. The other fear is that this atmosphere of mutual admiration society between Trujillo and Carter means they're going to try and pinch everything rolling thru Panama. Whatever the reason, they feel Jack is going to roll. They really wanted you badly for this one, but *ce la vie*..."

I pushed his words around, and didn't feel good. "So, the Weasel is loose down south? If they find he's still in Panama City will they try and clip him?"

"Either or. They have a guy in place right now for either option."

Now I was scared, "And the option of keeping Jack quiet too?" Clovis just sort of pursed his lips and wiggled his head a bit. The eye flutter was obvious. "What the fuck does that mean, Clovis?"

"Well, this guy is on standby for any event, and the guards are easily bribed." He said it too matter of factly.

"He's fucking family!"

"He knew what he was doing. There could be and obviously now, there are consequences. C'mon Remy, you were hipped to all prior to your excursion. There are dangers involved."

"He's family," I said coldly.

"He also cost many people a sizable amount of money and product."

"Well, did anybody give *them* the *talk* before investing in the smuggling of high grade cocaine that things may go south and they could lose everything?" I sneered.

He dodged that one.

I continued, "What about the Weasel angle, that he flipped on Jack. Doesn't that absolve Jack?"

"Jack is inside, doesn't matter the cause. He knows all of us. He has information."

We paused when the waitress came back, asked if we needed anything and being told we were good went back behind the counter.

"Jack will take the drop. I want two-thousand five hundred dollars from you to help and to keep Jack above water. If he's buoyant, you all needn't worry. Let him feel as if he's drowning, he'll grab the point of a sword to stay afloat. Okay? That should be a drop in the bucket for you, yes?"

He went thru his eye and clucking routine as I ate. "Let me think, talk to Meredith."

"What the fuck does she have to do with any of this?"

"We're married Remy. Because you don't tell your dusky jewel everything doesn't wash with my life."

"Don't go there."

"Then you don't go there." He raised his eyebrows, and I agreed inside he was right.

"Sorry, I was out of line. And her name is Sylvia."

"Sylvia, where for art thou, Sylvia?" He said in a bogus accent.

"Mocking me will take us to a place you don't like."

"Sorry. Where were we?"

"I want assurances Jack isn't on the chopping block, and I also want to know if there's a finders fee for the Weasel, if he's in PC"

"I can advocate for him yea. It may not change anything, and I'll ask about that too. Can you trust Nico at all? Younger than you guys and always a citizen."

"Yes, he's about all you can count on. Solid, stand up and will relay any and all messages."

"Okay, if you say so. Thru and thru his heart is blue." He laughed at his lame rhyme. I wanted to punch him.

"What's your theory?"

"I think the Weasel was turned and had him dropped. We had extra eyes at the airport and he saw the Weasel pull off what he thought was a signal"

"Duplicitous little fucker."

"You should've killed him when you wanted to back when."

At that I drifted away a little…I took a thru and thru in a brief exchange with an NV patrol in a howling rainstorm. We literally ran into each other like turning a corner in a noisy intersection and bumping into an old friend. Standing in the downpour, there was a pause as we realized the situation, our bodies rotating and turning sideways offering smaller targets on autopilot and before the signal from the brain was even sparked. I had my 16 at the ready while their AKs were slung but recovering quickly. I took out the first two guys in line and was throwing myself into the bush sideways when I felt a stinging on my right side. The survivors, no doubt were pulling their fallen buddies out, laying down fire in retreat. The short bursts of their AK's almost like music as they diddied. I knew they were in high aqua mode.

I did the hasty zumbago and zigzagged back in the direction of the platoon, which no doubt had heard my 16 and return fire. I knew my compass heading back yet took my time in getting there in case I had some pathfinders behind me and I didn't want to lead them right to my platoon. I had no idea how large their force, as I had only seen the first few guys before the exchange. By the time I came back in, the 1st Lt. was shitting himself having heard the gunfire but was being held in check by Hicks the gunny, who told him to shut the fuck up and called the Doc for me. In the soaking rain I hadn't noticed my entire blouse on the right hand side where I felt the sting, was soaked in my blood.

"Dumb ass Greek." Gunny Hicks grunted. The 1st Lt. regained composure and as the corpsman and a few other guys who covered us with ponchos went to work on me, had me describing the action in detail. No extractions in this soup, and with two holes in me patched with a fine blast of M that he wrote on my forehead so folks taking me off the bird would know I was hopped up, the doc and another lance corporal did a fireman's carry until we hit a stretch of open terrain. The rain had even let up, so Hicks allowed the 1st Lt. to call in a bird. Gunny Hicks told me to get my ass back pronto. He always said that to everyone, even the guys he knew were dying.

I ended up getting an infection at the BAS. Someone probably scratched his ass before changing my dressing and I ended up in the NavHosp in Saigon. It wasn't a good time. Guys were doped up to the gills all over the place and never wanting to return to the line. On and off I'd started reading the *Iliad* and *The Odyssey* during my tour. Both paperbacks I had were pretty watermarked and in places moldy. The Hospital had a good hardback of *The Odyssey* so I indulged. I'd made up my mind if I could get thru them while there in Viet Nam, if I finished both I'd make it home okay.

I knew I was short and almost ready to rotate back to the world but had put that out of my head. I was hooked up to an IV and stretched out on my rack at the Hospital and with this time on my hands I was good to go with the *Odyssey*. I was in the home stretch. Odysseus had wasted the suitors, reclaimed his wife and bed and was home free. But I wasn't. In a fever dream all of the dead I'd seen, known or dispatched paid me a visit. I was in the underworld like Odysseus had been when he met all the dead warriors from the battles of Troy; those guys from numerous patrols that died in the bush or after being med-evaced. Yea, and my NV and VC buddies too. I woke up shaking, feverish and full of the creeps. Best not to dream from the *Odyssey* anymore. Entertaining ideas of my end of tour and my detachment date, which coincided with my hospital stay. And so that was the end of my first tour, while in recovery in Saigon and thinking of all those guys who were history, as much as Troy was. I just stayed after my release from sickbay and I shipped over in the hospital. Before I left I was awarded a purple heart and a bronze star. When I returned Gunny just looked at me and shook his head.

"Asshole. This isn't mythology. You're not immortal."

I told him it was and I am. But he was right to call me an asshole because I was swept up in a moment I couldn't describe or express in any term. To me it was living mythology. For me every day was a journey from Troy. But I'd stopped thinking like Achilles after my standoff in the rain. Time to start thinking like Odysseus; get creative!

"I thought you were smarter Karras." I probably hear his voice in my ear saying that daily like an alarm clock. Gunny Hicks was honcho for three more months and then he cycled back, meeting his wife in Hawaii as he was destined to K-Bay for a school and then re-assignment. I was promoted to buck sergeant and transferred to a recon platoon farther north. I saw him before I mustered out at Pendleton, drinking his booze, listening to his music.

After catching a helo up country I was met at Fire Base Godzilla by my new Platoon OIC and Gunny after checking in. Over a beer, before the officer came on deck, Gunny Taylor asked after Hicks, how he was doing, as they'd come up together and attended recon training. Never offering anymore than a matchbook description I told him Hicks was well, on his way to Wahoo. Taylor looked at his zippo lighter with a Recon Symbol on it that he probably purchased from some geedunk in Saigon or Olongapo that he kept flipping back and forth, pursing his lips thinking.

"He said you were good people, level and could be counted on, Karras. That's good enough for me. The first lieutenant is an Academy guy and it took about four months to extract his head from his ass and now he's a pretty good bush marine." He finally lit his cigarette. "Do you smoke dope?"

"No. Do I need to?" I laughed.

"Up here, it helps." And then he said quietly, "Officer on deck," as the OIC walked in as we were standing.

"At ease, assholes."

I came out of my funk when Clovis shook my shoulder.

"Can I count on you, Remy?"

"Do I have to smoke dope?"

He had aggravation written all over his face. "Do what the fuck you think you need to do. Jesus, sometimes I think the jarheads fucked you and Francois into omelets!"

"Should I throw you off the roof?" I smiled. The memory of Gunny Taylor had faded. Much the same way the Gunny had, fading quietly into a morphine coma and then dying after taking a full round in the chest. His memory made my appetite fade. Clovis was making it fade as well. I didn't like his casual 'bye bye' attitude towards Jack, especially when I knew he could never in his life pull a trigger, ever. I looked him in the eye.

"I'm not sure all those fucking he-men with the exception of Francois could do time in a Latin jail and not think of snitching their own mothers out, okay?"

He laid his hands on the table, palms up. "I will tell them."

"Thank you."

"Meredith sends her love." He smiled.

I got up leaving my check. I walked out, wondering if I should clip him and his wife.

I hadn't planned on spending the night, and as PSA had flights every hour, I just drove back to the airport. If I had feared for Jack before, I really did now. What did it mean, they had a guy in place? Was he there? Was he a local they kept on retainer or was he some wet work guy from the Bay Area the Boys used like Justin? I felt a minor twinge of guilt in not dropping in on my folks, but they would somehow tie me to Nick's trip to Panama and I'd have to start lying my ass off again. I just wanted to get home and sleep.

The entire drive to the airport I thought of Dominic singing to his wife. Mel Torme, the Velvet Frog. Poor Dominic. I hoped Angela took all that skimmed cash and ran to Florida.

Doc Krinberg

Chapter 27

When they found Nick's body, he had been dead for over 48 hours. He was tied to a chair in the hotel room; arms behind him, nude except a pair of socks. The room had been tossed and there were obvious road maps of a B&E gone badly. There wasn't a penny left in the room and most of his clothes and articles were missing. He was paid up until the end of the week and in the timeline I reconstructed, he had been there two days. He had crammed in visits to Mairanos and Jack. I had a message on my phone machine and it was Nick's voice saying simply, 'He's here.' And that was it. The last person to see him alive had placed the muzzle of a small caliber weapon against his temple. He would've sat there until his bill wasn't settled but he had defecated and with the AC in the room shut off, a maid poking her head in due to the smell in the hallway, regardless of the Do Not Disturb sign threw up on discovering him.

My aunt was hospitalized and my uncle had moved into the spare room at my folks. I made arrangements to fly down, letting Matranga know the details up to a point, leaving Jack's visit to the Modelo out of the picture. Being what he termed a 'modern boss' he made a big deal out of 'allowing' me the grace. I had booked a direct flight and a consulate guy would try and meet me so we could expedite matters; help with the disposition, release of the body for transit back to California, and it would be commercial so there was a cost to that as well. I intended to just flog my BankAmerica card and also relieve Jack of some walking around money from his safe deposit. My dad was setting up the funeral arrangements and I'd call him before I left Panama with Nick so we didn't have to hang out at LAX in a cargo area. Clovis' folks called and had given the obligatory 'whatever you need' but that was code for 'leave us out of it, sorry for your loss.' I called Clovis from a pay phone while still in SF.

"Someone is going to get fucked where they breathe. Understand?"

"I'm brokenhearted. It was a robbery they say. Jesus, Remy, its Central America. It isn't like Pico and fucking Sepulveda."

"He left me a message, Clovis."

There was a long pregnant pause, "Yesss…?"

"The Weasel is there. I had described him to Nico and he sent me a phone message. The whole scene, the way they found him sounds staged. More like an extraction of info than a robbery. So listen, I want you to have something for me when I come down to LA. I'll need to stop there to get all the information for the funeral arrangements, pick up at LAX and all that depressing shit BECAUSE NICO IS FUCKING DEAD!" I couldn't help shouting into the phone. "Remember when our folks would go the Vegas and we all stayed at Yia Yia's when she lived in Santa Monica? They would always bring home those silver dollars?"

"Yes, I do."

"Well Jack and I would spend them on Topps baseball cards and whatever shit as fast as we could. Fucking Nico *saved* every dollar. He wasn't like us. This should not have happened. And don't tell anyone I'm armed."

"I understand. I'll get what you want." I hung up. He'd know I needed something small and powerful.

Later Elihu called my flat as I was packing and putting a dark suit in a garment bag, I didn't feel like talking.

"Remy, I'm sorry to hear about your cousin. Condolences." His *sotto voce* trying to soothe me, failing.

"Right. Thanks. I'm packing right now Eli," I said briskly.

"I want to make a contribution before you leave. Is that all right? When are you leaving?"

I had an evening flight and didn't need to leave for a couple or three hours.

"I see. I'm having Mona drop by in like thirty minutes to give you something. Clovis asked me to pick up an item you wanted."

"That'll be fine." But I was pissed. Just like Clovis to hand it off to someone else and breach Op Sec.

He continued, "Our mutual friends in Marin send their condolences as well, said bon voyage."

I hung up on him. Yea, I bet the D-boys were just crying into their beer over a jailed mule's brother being clipped. I needed to talk to Sylvia who had fallen thru the cracks in all of this. She was working nights and luckily that made it easier to detach and disappear for a few days.

"Is it that bad?" She asked yawning as I had woke her out of a dead sleep.

"Yes, its pretty bad. My cousin in jail? His younger brother went to see him and was robbed and murdered." Just saying it sounded unreal and her gasp made me feel his death even more. Brought it back into clear focus.

"Baby, I'm so sorry. God, yes just be careful and call me when you get back, okay?"

I let a few seconds slip by, then said in almost a whisper, "I love you, Sylvia."

She chuckled lightly, " 'Bout time you told me, Greek."

"You're right, 'bout time. Listen, if I'm not back in a week, there's a key to my flat with the older guy on the first floor and there'll be an envelope on the kitchen table. Got that? I told him your name and said you looked like Foxy Brown."

We laughed and she just said okay, didn't ask why. Definitely a keeper.

But I knew I wasn't.

Chapter 28

The lawyer was a professional. He must've represented about a thousand drug cases, foreigners, locals and adventurers of all stripes. Senor Marainos was himself well known and I wasn't in the least surprised the Boys had his business card.

His office was plush, but not overtly so. It didn't look quite like a high-end whorehouse bar or a law library but it was easy to see by the woodworking and the odd art piece that he was well funded. In his late fifties, he had probably seen it all and knew his shit when working a bought plea bargain or sentencing. He had those tired iguana eyes that blinked slowly and moved even slower.

"You have something for me?" He smiled.

"Yea, I do, but lets talk first. Tell me, please, about Nick's visit." He had already paid his condolences when I came in and had shaken hands. He also submitted it was a double tragedy since Jack was incarcerated blah blah blah. He explained that Nick was very frightened for his brother and wanted the best to be done.

"Did he give you the cash?"

"He did, yes. So the robbery was a failure and unfortunately your primo, your cousin, paid the consequences." Marainos had a defined, upper class accent. His Spanish I heard when speaking to his secretary as I came in sounded almost Castilian.

"Did you two discuss an outline, an itinerary you wanted to follow for Jack? Court dates, pay-offs, etc." He gave me a hurt look as if I made him feel bad at mention of 'pay-offs.' I looked at him and again just stayed business, "Don't. Don't lets play that that elephant isn't in the room, please. Don't lets play fiddle fuck, okay? No hurt feelings or pretenses. I'm not Nick, and by the grace of the Great Green Frog I didn't need you back in the day." And I had an overwhelming wave of guilt as I realized how wrong I had been to allow Nick or anyone else to come down here. This was, I felt, on Jack and I exclusively. Marainos' manner changed and switching to business mode outlined what was a standard practice. In the end it would be around $27,500-30,000, not to include what had already been spent in regards to food, safety and arranging people in this strange pipeline. Then there were the needed incentives and incidentals, *por favor*. No ifs, ands, or buts. Fucking muleskinners from Jump Street. We hadn't even started the judicial process.

I told him I also needed to insure Jack wasn't hurt, ass-raped and had a solid food connection he liked. Getting one wasn't a problem, but if your food sucked, why keep paying? I also needed to obtain a mailing address that could allow for his mail to not be searched or confiscated and was told by this mouthpiece that all mail to him was privileged and he could allow Jack this library time under the auspices or attorney-client discussions. But of course, there was an extra whack for that. He agreed readily to help in all he could do, and I had to hold down my mirth at that one. Then I asked him the one question I needed to know; had the Weasel initiated this business with him. When I asked, his lizard eyes fluttered a tad, and lighting a cigarette, blew smoke at the ceiling fan and said he had been contacted by a Mr. Berberian, who while never meeting him personally left with his secretary a sum of cash to initiate a 'business arrangement' with Jack. I smiled standing, offered my hand. He stood to meet me.

"*Mucho gusto,* Senor Marainos. I'm glad to have you in our corner. Can you arrange my visit to the Carcel Modelo tomorrow morning?" I smiled.

"Si, si. Me alegra haberte conocido así. es un placer hacer negocios con un hombre que es versado en cómo se hacen los negocios, Senor Karras. We shall make sure your primo is well taken care of and we can start the judicial ball rolling early next week when he is finally formally charged." Smiling, his teeth were a dark yellow from decades of cigarettes.

Having a date with the consulate guy to help return Nico to California I cut short the mutual admiration of crooks society with the mouthpiece. I also had the knowledge now that the Weasel had done his job, and got Jack help; he also probably saved him from rotting in the 'pig pen' Mona described. Why would a guy who had turned him, help him? I needed to head back to the hotel to shift colors as I was sweating like a whore in church. The humidity was just oppressive and I joked with myself I would have savage flashbacks to 'Nam and start trying to bite fenders on cars. The fact that the taxi I was in had no AC and smelled like 45 years of Brylcream and cigars didn't help.

When I walked into the lobby there was a guy in a lightweight leisure suit that reeked Fed. I stopped, turned towards the bar and tapped the end of my cigarette as leisure suit walked in, trying not to look like a donkey dick. He finally came over and sat two stools away and snapped his fingers at the bar tenders who had ignored me pretty good up to this point, flirting with two cocktail waitresses.

"Can I buy you a drink?" he asked, not looking at me.

"That's okay, you're not my type." I smiled back.

"Nick didn't play hard to get…Remy." His voice while friendly, took on an edge.

"First, take my cousin's name out of your mouth. Second, Just tell it.

I'm not here on vacation, but you would know that." I lit my cigarette and blew smoke at him, smiling.

"I had a long talk with him about his brother, and he was amenable, saw where his brother's interests were also ours."

"When did you talk? Before or after he saw Marainos? Just cut to the chase, buddy."

"Before. We had breakfast his first morning, and like I say he was relieved we talked. Maybe you should be too." The bartender finally strolled over and leisure suit asked for a beer. I had a ginger ale in the can, and stuffed a lime down inside it.

"What's your name, or are introductions too hard for you? I have no clue who you are and you sit here and tell me you sold my cousin a bill of goods in how he should conduct business with his own brother." I drained half of my ginger ale, and stood up.

"Wait, wait, brother..." He extended his hand and placed it on my forearm. "Please, sit down." He pulled a card. I turned it over; Don Elias, DEA. "I've been around since '68, when we were the Bureau. I've been here for two years. I think that's two years after *you* flew south wasn't it?" He smiled. "Water under the bridge, amigo. I can help Jack, but he needs to help us. I don't need to tap dance with you Remy, do I? You told Ni... your cousin all the right things, but he'd never been to the dance before. I mean you know the dance, and well, so let's get down to it. He needs us. We can have him home in a month if he plays ball."

"A month? Are you going to pay Marainos double?" I laughed. "And if Jack doesn't? If we allow it to run thru the courts?"

"Then all you do is grease the greasy palms of all these fuckers here, starting with Senor Marainos, who owns a beautiful villa, has a 17 year old mistress and as he plunders your family's bank accounts the cartel guys keep him on retainer as well."

"Man's gotta eat. And?" I could just picture my sadly departed Nico being swayed by this double knit fuck, distrusting the Latin drug lawyer over an American.

"You're going to see him tomorrow yes?" He was too eager. Two years in the tropics should've slowed him down, but this guy was hyper, maybe behind an eight ball. He knew I wouldn't bite or even think of it until after I had talked to Jack.

I shrugged my shoulders, beads of sweat running down my spine, "I have a meeting with a consular guy about transit of Nick from the funeral home to the airport and to accompany it. I'll see his brother after that. I'm in mourning, Mr. Elias, this is a man who was like a brother to me, and I'm not in the mood to fucking play Five-O for you. Now, if you have any modicum of decency, you'll leave me alone for now. I have your card. If I don't call you, just stay fucked off, okay?"

He looked at me. I could see it finally sank in and could see him reconfiguring the situation, the new angles. "I understand. Pardon my exuberance, I thought I could help your family, who by now are in a lot of pain."

"Don't. Don't play that." I got up this this time for good.

He turned in his chair, rotating to me as I walked around him, "I was Marines, too."

"No doubt some office pogue whose neck would snap if the OIC turned a corner too sharply.

His voice at my back wasn't too convincing when he said, "You'll be calling. And, oh, by the way, Mr. Berberian says 'hello'."

I felt like he had hit me with a bat as I walked away, but I just kept walking, cadence coming into my head, the old discipline; *...Aint no use in going home, Jody got your girl and gone, I'm gone get a three day pass, I'm gone kick old Jody's ass...*Yea buddy. Was it real bait, throwing the

Weasel at me or just throwing shit against the wall? Whatever it was, I was in the elevator then and cursing reality when the doors shut. Was it for real, or just a poke to make me jump? Was the Weasel an agent or had they flipped him after a bust? This was like a chessboard with multiple moves; many variations unknown. You could play fifty sides against each other, up and down, and forty-nine would be bogus. I left the elevator and even in the cool of the hotel, the ankle holster was wet from my conversation with Don Elias, if that was even his name.

The next two hours were depressing. I almost felt like I was back at MCRD being processed with the entire procedure swirling around Nick and the 'robbery' it was drowning by paperwork. The consular guy was joined on and off by other people, one blatantly a spook who asked me about Jack and if he had any political associations with juntas or communists. I told him flatly, Jack is my cousin, and I can't read his mind. He gave me that 'fuck you, lightweight' smile before he diddied.

The most depressing news was the true facts. He was found tied to a chair, and had been beaten first, abused, and then a small caliber pistol placed against his left temple. This part of the story had been left out of the version that floated up north, sparing his parents any more pain than they could handle. I kept wondering what he had told Marainos. Had he discussed at length proposals made to him by Elias? If so, what did this confession bear? This was a key for me. It must have been dynamite to waylay him. Or was his discussion with Jack eavesdropped on? Mr. DEA may be the man I need to talk to.

After all the paperwork was done, and the flights were synced with fees paid I needed a real drink, and needed it badly. I had free time now as I would see Jack in the morning, but I was having problems navigating in the heat, and the flying teeth that found me appetizing. I felt like I could shower five times a day. It hadn't been this bad in Lima, but I had also been down when the weather was better. This was like being in Olangapo or Tanse Nhut. I never missed the humidity and it was a big reason I lived where I did. I could open my window on Hugo and some nights taste the ocean in the fog. The coolness. I would open the window after lovemaking with Sylvia and just allow the cool air to cover me. She asked me, shivering and burrowing into the covers why and I just answered 'the war' and she let it go. I needed that cool air now. I also couldn't take the gun to the carcel as they would shake me down hard. In the room, I pulled my shirt off and threw it, wet, onto the chair. I went into the head and started a shower as I stripped off totally and placed the pistol under a towel that was thrown over a towel rack, and stepped in.

He was sitting on the shitter and holding my pistol. At least he had left me my towel.

"Hello Arthur."

"Hello, Remy. Sti-sti-still surfing?"

"Not too much anymore. Have to drive down to Santa Cruz for any good waves and I don't have a car anymore. Still chasing jailbait?" I took the towel slowly and started rubbing my skin. He smiled and I noticed his new teeth, much whiter.

"Not so much." Still smiling.

"I'm starting to get bored. Talk, shoot or leave."

"I didn't ki-kill him. I know why you're here and I know what you want to find me for, but it isn't me. I could've ki-killed you already, just on fucking p-principle but I didn't. Your family has suffered enough tr-tragedy and I'm not without empathy. But you're wrong about me. You and I met under a very different situation, in a microcosm, and you don't know me."

"Then tell me who." I wrapped the towel around my waist and leaned against the shower wall, my arms folded.

"I'm not sure, but I do know its someone who isn't cartel or government. I have a gut feeling but I can't p-rove it. When I can, I'll let you know." He raised his eyebrows as if it were a question he'd just asked.

"Okay, this interlude has me at a disadvantage and asking a lot of questions inside. Do you know what Nick was going to tell Jack?"

"Maybe. The DEA guy braced him first thing; the same guy who tagged you in the b-bar, and then he went to Marainos. Then he went to Jack. And then," he sighed, "he was d-dead. I'm thinking the lawyer and someone else who takes his marching orders from NorCal. But hey, that's just me."

I thought about it, and it made sense. They even told me they 'had eyes' here and sent someone to bat cleanup if need be. "Nick made you. I had given him your description and he let me know. I'm tired, Arthur. It's been a long day. I see Jack in the morning" I said with finality.

"You can't take this." He placed the pistol on the sink. "When you see him, te-tell him, I didn't cause him to drop."

"There are a lot of arrows pointing at you Arthur. You disappear and freak everyone out, and then you're back. Fucking Fuqua tried to bail on the whole run after your intermission. Lots of red flags, old man."

"D-Did he now?" He stood. "How convenient, isn't it? Say hello to Jack. Tell him it wasn't me." He dropped a matchbook on the sink next to the gun and walked out. I probably could've jumped him in my towel and pinned him to talk more but I watched him leave the room and shut the door quietly. I just leaned back against the wall, running my hand thru my hair and watched. Finally I pushed myself off the wall and wiping off the mirror noticed a doodle he had left in the bottom corner. It was a little 'J.'

Fucking Weasel. I believed him. But I knew I was only getting a fraction of the story.

Even though it was early, I was about to drop dead. I called up room service for some eggs, bacon and whisky. Then I passed out hard.

Doc Krinberg

Chapter 29

The jail, while called 'modelo' was not a fun looking place. I reported to a check in area and signed my name and also wrote down Marainos, as legal advocate. Reading the lawyer's name the desk officer smiled and rubbed his thumb and forefinger together. Next, I was led into a secure area and searched, then taken to a visitor's center; I sat and waited for my cousin Jack to appear.

I never really knew why Jack dabbled in the felonious world when he did so well at the dealership. He was good at sales and had that knack to make guys in midlife crisis really want that '59 Morgan Plus 4 or the 'Steve McQueen' Jag. His flat in Noe was in a renovated Victorian that had even appeared in a magazine. He had a guy in Chinatown that made his suits and with no steady women in his life pretty much banged his way thru Union and Clement Street bars. And now the Modelo. The Waco as the inmates deemed it. As he came thru the adjoining door I had to look twice. He looked fucking miserable. This was not the Beau Brummel I knew. He looked like one of those guys down on Hallidie Plaza hustling butts. And he was also in mourning.

"Please tell me you'll take care of things? Please Remy." He had finished all his crying before I got there, and his voice had that hollow, metallic tone; no spirit left inside the vessel.

I didn't want to dwell on Nico so just asked about the now, and how things were and if he was getting along. What he needed immediately and how was Marianos, in his opinion.

"That fucking thief bastard grows fat from guys like me!" He leaned in and I lit his cigarette. The one I had given him.

"Do they let you keep smokes where you're at now? Any possessions?"

He rolled his eyes, "Where I'm at now, yes. You can send books, mags, cigs, lice shampoo, and I can even trade for other things as well. Fucking insane. Remember when you read 'Papillon?' We're there. The first place I went to was total bedlam. There was no segregation, everyone was mixed in…murderers, arsonists, assbandits, rapists, dopers, Latinos and me. No beds, just a stone floor. Showers? Fucking one bathroom that had two pipes coming out of the wall and Remy, so many of the fuckers had dysentery and the shitter was one hole in the middle of the floor and it was fucking alive! The floors were crawling with goddamn intestinal worms these poor fuckers were passing. Remy, it was insane!" His voice was almost cracking. "Some of these guys didn't even have shoes and they were just wading thru worms. I've never seen anything this disgusting, as guys were squatting over this hole, shitting guts and worms out and the stink, oh for fucking Chrissakes I was there for three days and then Marainos got me transferred here to the Waco. I'm not even sure what that cost but it was worth every penny. The morning they pulled me out some guy was murdered by another." His voice cracked here, and I knew he had turned back to Nico in his thoughts at mention of the inmate's murder. "Why did they kill him? Was it the fucking Boys? Weasel? God, Remy, he wasn't a threat. Why?" He put his forehead in his hands and cried. I let him go on as much as he needed.

"Did anything weird go on at the buy? Was Berberian acting squirrelly?"

He wiped his eyes and nose. "No. Everything was fine. It went swimmingly. Lima was smooth and the set up was fine. It was when we bottle necked into Panama City. They knew. I was a mark. Fucking set up. Nick..." He started crying again.

"Have any DEA guys been in to interview you? Besides the State department guys?"

"One guy. Told me to roll on everyone and they'd try and spring me before the system drained my parents. Are they okay? Please tell me they aren't selling the farm to keep me in cigarettes, street tacos and *mondongo*. I feel like shit for what they're going thru." He looked at me with a deprecating smile. "I really fucked up hard didn't I? Hey, did you go to my flat?"

"Yea, I did. Listen, I'm trying to get this whole thing done by underwriting it with supplemental cash from the Board and concerned others. Don't worry about the money. And as stated, I took five K from your deposit box and threw it on the pile. I added $2500, and I got Clovis to also kick in that much, so you're in fat city. I'm going to try and get a jolt from the Boys as well and yea, your folks are a fuck story, and I won't lie. Tell me more about this DEA guy."

"You took five thousand from me? This guy, he came in before Nico flew down. Friendly, cajoling...then threatening. I told him to leave me alone, and I acted on my own, nobody else. He leaves me a pack of Salems and tells me he'll be back. What's the scene in the City?"

"A grim tableau and bad moods. They think the Weasel made a deal. Just speculation."

"Then why would he help me, set up Marainos and spend money after I dropped?"

"Good point. They didn't tell me that up north. I only learned it down here." I thought for a moment. "Can you hold any cash in here?"

"Nooo...I'd be murdered if anyone knew. I'm in segregation now, me, a guy from Kentucky, two Europeans and a South African. One of the euros is a fag from Belgium who is getting out toot sweet. We do mingle with some Panamanians who are waiting to go to the island, but we're not with the psychos like in that holding area. These guys going to the island will never be heard of again, so they let them chill out beforehand." He sighed, looking around. "My new digs." He laughed weakly.

"Yes, beautiful, yet slimacious." I laughed. "Let's get thru this. You need to stay strong and stand up. There is considerable doubt from other people with a concern here. Yes? Whatever they offer you, turn it down. Let it take its time with money and Marainos. This is a system. A certain amount of time needs to be served so they don't look like a shakedown company. If you roll, things will get ugly fast and you'll be marked. You wont make it out of here, Jack, and I'm telling you this so you get it. Do your time until we buy you out. You have to make your own time, day to day. Understand?"

Tears again, "Yes." He was quiet, just shaking his head. "Where are they going to have the funeral?"

"Santa Monica, service at the Orthodox church there."

The guard coughed loud. I looked at him and he lifted his chin to indicate I needed to wrap it.

"I have to go. I need to tighten the strings here and there and take Nico home. Remember what I told you."

"I'm glad you're taking him, Remy. Please send my folks my love and apologies. I'm sorry. I wrote a letter but I don't even know if it got out. Can you check?" He just sounded busted up inside, miserable.

"Okay. Tell that prick if you need anything to have him get in touch with me promptly. Take care Jack, I know you can do this."

"Do you?"

"Yes." Then he gave me a weak smile and went for the Conrad. "Exterminate the brutes."

I smiled back, "The horror...the horror." We laughed at that. It was an old bit we played since reading the novella in high school. I got up and gave him the carton of cigarettes they let me bring in. I took out a ten dollar bill, folded it into thirds and gave it to the guard, smiling he touched the brim of his cap. Then I remembered something.

"Jack." He turned before going thru the gate to his secured area. "Don't say anything to your cell mates either. No details, nothing. Talk about your job in the city, or pussy—yea? No life story, no relatives, no names."

He nodded. My paranoia was flying high. And seriously, why wouldn't it?

My return to the hotel was uneventful, but again I was dead tired. The emotional drain with Jack took a toll and I needed a drink, a nap, something. On the horizon were massive dark clouds, and the wind direction was just right. A thunderstorm was inbound and at least a quick break in the heat was due. I didn't need any more visits but I was wrong. The DEA guy was again lurking, probably having shadowed me to the Carcel Modelo.

"Aren't there any number of fucking traffickers to pick from?" I frowned.

"Yea, but none involves murder and so many moving parts." He smiled.

"Fuck off, Elias. We're not here for your entertainment. I haven't shit to say to you."

He gave me a *tsk tsk*. "Come on, Remy. We should be pals. I'm a good guy."

"Really? I'm under the impression you muddied the waters in my cousin's head and he panicked and wanted to tell Jack to roll on his associates. That close to it? And if so, you probably helped get him killed. So diddy mao, pogue."

"Unlike you, he listened to reason. But you're a tough guy, hard case. Still in recon."

I just walked by him and went to the maître de hotel, pointed at Elias and told him that man had asked me to attend a donkey show. Then I went to the elevators. I wondered who would be in my room today, but it was empty. On the nightstand was the matches Berberian had left me. It was a club called 'El Bufo Negro.' The Black Toad. Written in the corner of the inside cover was '9-nightly.'

Maybe I should've gone there last night.

Chapter 30

Mona had dropped by my flat just as Elihu had said she would.

"Hmmm, I like your place Remy. How you say, very Marine? Very masculine." She went and sat on the couch in front of my Gauguin reproductions. "I'm impressed."

"What do you have for me?" I wanted her in and out.

"You weren't very nice to me the other night. But you can make amends." She smiled, unbuttoned her coat, and pulling it open wore a see thru blouse of very light blue. "Do you like my new blouse?"

"The piece, Mona. I'm packed and I need to stash it away. C'mon. My cousin was murdered, his brother is in jail and I'm not thinking about scrogging right about now."

She pouted, put her hand into her oversized shoulder bag and came out with a 7.62 Tokarev with a wrap around ankle holster, one clip in. Where did he get this shit?

"Are you going to kill someone, Remy?" She said huskily. "Really... tell me."

I rolled my eyes. " Is that an aspect of ontology you want to discuss? I need it for protection. Thank you. Now please, I have to finish and then hit the airport."

She seemed to have gotten it finally, and backed off. " It is an interesting book. Elihu said you were a badass in Viet Nam. Force Recon,

SOG."

"Not really. Why is it people you don't like tell the best lies about you?" Elihu was like a drunk, embellished shit and said too much.

"Why don't you like Elihu?"

"Besides being besties with my loser cousin Clovis or the obvious reasons, do you wish me to dig deeper?" I raised an eyebrow. "Why do you?"

She smiled, running a finger along the back of my couch, "That's a good question."

"I'll stop asking questions based on my own ignorance. What else did Elihu say? Did he talk about Panama?"

"Noooo…" she said coyly, "why? Think there's more to this than meets the eye?"

"Mona, you would know more than anyone there's always more than meets the eye, neh?"

"You know I was in Saigon in 1965."

That caught my attention. "Why were you there?"

"I worked there." She said simply staring at my Gauguin's.

"Dancing?"

"No. I was assigned there. I used to work in Hawaii and then got transferred. And I was involved." She smiled, "He wasn't a marine, but I wasn't always a dancer. When I came home I had a couple of lost years"

She stood up in my living room, bra less and her nipples always erect, just poking at me. I shook my head at the entire scene and then I got angry. I took the two steps to her and grabbing her hard, squeezed them both until she finally let out a series of gasps. "Thanks Mona." I held up the Tokarev in the holster. "Tell Elihu I *owe* him."

She seemed to reenter the world slowly, "Damn! You still owe me, Remy." She still had her eyes shut and started massaging her breasts, as if to reshape them after my hands. "Yes, you do."

"See you on the flip side." And I started pushing her towards the door. I couldn't fuck her, so it was the only thing I could do. She was insanity, embodied. I still don't know why I wanted to hurt her. Or why I kept thinking about her. I also wondered what happened to her in Viet Nam. Lately, it was as if she was giving me a puzzle piece, just one at a time.

But was Elihu insane?

Doc Krinberg

Chapter 31

At nine p.m. I was sitting in the Black Toad and nursing a beer. I had already blown off the entreaties of two girls and I could see why the Weasel liked this place. The girls working it were high school age at the very least. Some things never changed.

He slithered into the seat next to me, and after ordering a beer leaned a little away from me and said, "That ankle holster is a little obvious."

I laughed, "You're not that good. You knew I'd have an ankle holster, saw it when you came into the room."

"Elihu?"

"Yea."

"He's fond of them because he read about them once or saw a movie, I ca-can't remember. Strap one on him and he'd break out in hives."

"So why am I here?"

"I had hoped you would be last night. To find your cousin's ki-killer."

"Why am I believing you?"

"You don't have to like me, Remy, and we have bad b-blood between us, but what do I gain by lying?"

"That visit in the bathroom…the 'J.' Is that Justin?"

"Yes. Nick was an easy mark, sorry, but he was. Justin hasn't found me yet cuz this is all different for him, he's a Pa-panama City virgin. But I know where he is. He came down with his wife and baby—good cover.

But he's not connected or as mobile as he needs to be and I've lived here and down in Lima for twenty years. Want to know where he is?"

"Yes." I said flatly.

"He's at the Sheraton, room 1404.

"And then?"

"I don't know," he shrugged, "this is the first time I've been in this po-po-position. All my other mules made it home and I've never been hunted before. If you can't separate him from his wife and ki-kid?"

"Play it as it lays and let the devil take the hindmost. "I dropped a sawbuck on the bar. "Thanks. You know how to get in touch with me before tomorrow. I'm also listed in the SF white pages."

"Listen, I c-c-cant stay down here. There's nothing for me to do now. I have to be up north. That's where things will happen." He wrote down a number. "If I'm there, c-call this. I've written it backwards. C-c-call once, hang up, and then c-call back. Got that?" I had a serious feeling I'd need this.

I walked out.

The Tokarev against my ankle felt heavy on my cab ride to the Sheraton. At the house phones I called 1404 and had a woman with an eastern European accent answer and tell me no, maybe I meant the last occupant.

So the info I got from Berberian was already stale. I'd maybe missed my window of opportunity the night before. Justin, wife and baby had checked out and trying to follow it up would be a waste. If the Weasel were on the level, then finding him in Northern Cali wouldn't be hard. Francois would probably help. Call in the Semper Fi chip on that one.

This is what Rauol Duke would term a savage failure. My trip here and attempting to tie loose ends while obtaining a modicum of payback for Nico was a bust. I did get to Jack but was it enough? Was it timely? There was still some doubt. I had greased the funeral home guys for the airport delivery and State had supplied a standard stainless steel casket for transport and stood by as I accompanied Nico to the airport, thru the customs guys and out to the plane. Sadly, the casket and I were thoroughly searched when we hit the wall there. I had dropped that piece and holster after returning from the Sheraton. No use in answering questions.

The flight crew knowing I was accompanying a family member home moved me up to an empty first class seat and appreciatively, I drank a lot. My only fear now was that the cable instruction the LA funeral home to meet us would be fucked up.

Chapter 32

LA was the nightmare I knew it would be. My aunt was sedated the entire time and held up by aunties and friends, uncles and my dad. This was an all hands on deck affair. Their mother, Yia Yia had been replaced more or less by her sister Constance who took the honorary roll of granny. I tried to dodge almost everyone and finally dragged Clovis into the den at my dad's house, which was hosting. I had tried to see him prior to the funeral but he had avoided me and out at the cemetery on Pico near the college was not the place to have an extended conversation about drugs and murder. When I finally pinned him down, I had to push his wife out of the room.

"Okay, everything you know, or think you know, Clovis." He sat down, and put his forehead in his palms.

"I'm trying to process this, Remy," he sighed.

Looking down at his head I wanted to put my cigarette out in the part of his hair. He was trying to process? Fucking Nico was dead and one of his fucking buddies was in the mix, if not one or all of the D-boys.

"Tell it Clovis, talk to me." I had to cool down or I'd end up beating him to death.

He sighed again, "I don't know what happened. Honest to fucking God I'm thinking it might've been one of the people on the other end, the Peruvians who maybe thought Nico was a liability after seeing a DEA guy.

That he had info on him." Then he looked up but avoided my eyes, "Or maybe it was the Weasel?"

When had I ever told him or anybody up north that Nico had talked to the guy Elias? The Weasel knew, but he wasn't talking to anybody.

The Weasel. I had a feeling Clovis would default to him; easy mark, and since he went AWOL before now a sweeter fall guy. I let that ride as I shook my head, as if in deep thought I didn't let on that I knew everything else or that Berberian and I had talked in Panama City. I didn't want Clovis to think anything else, but his fingering Weasel said plenty and mentioning the DEA said more.

I pushed his shoulder so he'd look at me, "Okay, that makes sense. Has anyone heard from or have any updates on him?"

Clovis stood up, feeling his spine again, no doubt. "No, into thin air. He could be hiding in Argentina with Mengele for all we know." He took out a cigarette, "We should go back, yea?"

"Yea." I opened the door and Meredith almost fell into the room. "I'll send you a transcript later," and walked out. I went straight to the booze.

My cousin Jennifer, wearing this super low cut black dress was mixing a drink. She turned to me.

"This is a real mess Remy. Both of those brothers." She said in a whisper, "Did you know Jack was a drug racketeer?"

"No." I picked up the whisky and poured a couple of fingers into a pony glass. Dropping the ice in I leaned in closer to her. "Did you?"

In shock she backed up, "NO! Why in hell would I know? Jesus, I've got enough on my plate trying to divorce that redneck *pusti* I married that became a pig. I haven't seen any of you in ages."

Jennifer was a year older than me and had attended Fairfax High. We used to kid her about living up in the Borscht Belt of Fairfax and Beverly Blvd. and finding a nice Jewish boy who was going to be a doctor, but she went to UCSB and married a blonde Baptist from Kentucky. I can remember her saying to me the last time we met over some holiday 'He's good looking, but I had no clue he was such a hick under it all. Who goes to UC Santa Barbara and votes Republican?'

I looked at my aunt sitting in between my folks. She and her husband immediately older; ancient, broke down. Jennifer's mom was fixing people plates of food. Behind her I could see kids in the yard. She turned to me.

"Remy, you look healthy. What do you do in San Francisco? Are you gay?"

"Mom!" Her daughter blushed.

I laughed, "No auntie, I work for the teamsters."

She rolled her eyes, "Ohhhh so you're a crook like that Bobby Hoffa?"

I smiled, "Jimmy Hoffa." I could imagine Jennifer melting throughout her entire life.

"Him too." She waved me off with a hand.

Jennifer was shaking her head. My aunt walked away. "God, its like All in the Family." She sighed.

"So are you staying with your mom?" Her dad, Harry, had died years ago. "Oh my God, no. I got a room at the Holiday Inn on Century. I need my privacy. I flew in from Phoenix."

"Right. Forgot you lived there."

She sipped her drink, "Are you staying here with your folks?"

"I planned on it. I'm a bit whacked out from flying to Panama and back."

"Do you have a car? She picked me up from the airport, and I'm ready to go."

"Yea, if you need a ride, let me know I can take you."

"Good, then let me say some goodbyes and let's go."

Five minutes later, after an explanation and kissing my aunt & mom I was driving my other cousin to her hotel near the airport.

Chapter 33

I probably used a little too much coke after returning to the City. I was starting to feel as if I needed it to take the edge off the day. I basically locked myself in the office at work and gave standing orders to leave me alone unless one of the 'corporate' guys came by. This lasted a few days and unfortunately Sylvia also paid for this funk. I had called her the day I returned and said I needed to keep my own counsel and while she acquiesced I could tell she wasn't happy. She mentioned being alone wasn't healthy and joked I needed a nurse. I got a call from Elihu to drop by and I never returned the call, but then thought better and returned it imploring I meet with *those* people to discuss Jack. My dad also called, but it was awkward and we both cut it short.

I also had a few things to do. I attended a local meeting casting a vote and a few other errands for my bosses, and another run by Jack's flat to validate that it had been searched. I had to laugh noticing the Playboy stack was moved and out of order. I also fell by his place of employment as they had fired him in absentia and I needed to clear all of his shit out of his small office. They gave me a final check, some hard looks and a gruff attitude. Searching inside his desk, I found a vial taped up under the underside of the desk corner that the Feds had missed; at least half a gram of blow. This was Jack's 'Sherlock' stash. And now it was mine. We used to joke about how Sherlock kept his coke stash private and only dived into it when he was behind the 8-ball or chilled out after a hard case.

Jennifer crossed my mind.

With all the nonsense blowing around me like a whirlwind I felt guilty as hell. I had to start taking stock in my errant and morally elastic behavior. In Jack's flat he had a huge poster of Bosch's *Garden of Earthly Delights* triptych and all I could picture, when staring at it was being eaten by a giant bird and shit out into a pot. That's where my soul was. Not being religious didn't mean I thought I was above eternal reprisals. I had hit a tipping point, flying to Panama with a piece to kill the Weasel, the interlude with the DEA guy who I should've killed for setting Nico up and then Los Angeles. I usually only used my Sherlock when working out a chess problem, or listening to jazz and blues but I had broken that barrier.

By the time I saw Sylvia, she told me I looked like utter fuck, and I did. The tide of guilt somewhat subsided and I felt I could live with resolve again. But I told her there was no way I could stay at her place so she made plans to see me. There was no way I wanted to draw any attention to her personal life and anyway, her fucking roommate Marta was crazier than a shithouse rat.

We went to Clement Street, across the park for dinner at a French place we liked and she carefully required that I tell her at my own speed about Panama and Los Angeles. I told her almost everything. I didn't know how she could process my cold bloodedly hunting down a guy in a foreign country, or irresponsibly taking methaquualone with my cousin. And not once. I couldn't lay all that on Ms. Sylvia Jones. Up the street at a club, the Mystic Knights of the Oingo Boingo were headlining so we caught that mayhem and then enjoyed a sweet night.

It got Jennifer out of my head.

The next day and I called Elihu on a pay phone across the street from the garage to a pay phone he used that was on Fillmore and Union. "And so?" I asked.

"WE need to talk about your sojourn down south, old boy. Also, there's a DEA guy who has been making the rounds of all of Jack's KA's; people at his work, guys he golfs with and a few women he dated." Elihu was in his Wm. F. Buckley white umbrage voice.

"How did they find them? I cleaned his Rolodex out of his pad and it was before they tossed it, the fed guys. They've been in and out. But I cleaned it."

Elihu sighed, "Yea but he also wrote things down at work, and left impressions on his office blotter. MY NUMBER, REMY! The fuckers came to my house!"

I smiled uncontrollably, imagining how *that* went and how in the world he didn't die of a fucking heart attack sitting there in front of his cocaine cereal bowl when the bell rang and Elihu going thru his face twitching gyrations. Thoughts like chess pieces—do I play this one? What space can this one go to? Do I say I wanted to buy a car from him…but hey, I also know his cousins. And did Mona do a quick costume change that would rock the Feds back on their heels, eyes on the candy?

I was still smiling when he asked me to come by as we needed to talk about that woman he wished to set me up with; the 'woman' our code for blow. I told him no meets at his house. I didn't wish to be seen there, and in the long run, he didn't want me there either. Not now.

"Use the theater gig," I told him.

"Agreed."

The theater gig meant hitting the Bijou porn theater on Market Street, then crashing the back exit and having a meeting at this dive we used in the past, the Shangri-La on Eddy. It still had tall backed booths that were dark and afforded privacy if you didn't mind what you sat in. I had taken a seat facing the door, getting there ahead of him.

"Tell me about Panama," he said. He looked like he might've gotten ahead of me and spent time in the Bijou. He took out a handkerchief, wiped his forehead, then spit on it and wiped the rim of his gimlet glass.

And I told him. But I left out the chapter where Arthur Berberian and I bonded and discussed things. I mentioned the DEA guy and the Latin shyster that held Jack's life in his hand.

"Think Jack can stand his drop?"

"Jesus. Yes, he can take it. Now that he's out of general population and in with other gringos, out of the hole. Can he see any help out of the Board?"

Elihu drank. "God damn this tastes awful. Remind me why we use this place?"

"Because you and Clovis like sitting in other men's semen?" I said smiling.

He frowned, "All right. So do you feel the DEA knows more than we think?"

"The DEA knows there's money in the Bay Area and I get the drift that a few of us are on the periphery of their radar. Seriously, you can't continuously do this shit without somebody noticing, or snitching. Get real. And then seeing Jack is from here and couldn't do it alone they're poking their noses in any hole they can smell. What did you tell them when they visited?"

"That I am Elihu Fuqua, the III, and that his older cousin and I have been friends for over thirty years, and as Jack is his family at times I send someone who is interested in an older classic car. I highlighted that my friends could afford *those* type of cars."

I shook my head. "Wow. Good call."

"Mona also *walked* in," he smiled.

"That must have derailed everything."

"She knows how to work a diversion." He leaned forward as if in pantomime. I didn't know why but when he said it I didn't like it. My eyes were accustomed to the dark now and I could see his face.

"I thought I glimpsed Justin down there, in Panama City…" I saw his eyes blink rapidly.

He stuttered like the Weasel, "J-Justin? East Bay Justin?"

"No. Justin. East Bay Justin is an Angel, Oakland Chapter, and he's serving a three-year jolt in Soledad for a free basing beef. The *other* Justin, you know, at the Sheraton with some hillbilly looking chick. I dropped by there to drink. Was he there in Panama?"

Rapid blinking, "Not to my knowledge. Haven't seen him in months. He just had a kid awhile back with this fucking teenage chick from Kentu…met her in Venice Beach." Shook his head. "I think she was a runaway."

"He's smart. Easy to control, and for what he does, she would never know and give good cover. Like 'hey baby, let's take a vacation, you me and the baby…' and while there *whack!* " I hit the table top when I said that, making him jump back.

"Well, he wasn't."

"But you said you hadn't seen him in months?" I asked calmly. Then I sighed. "Well, maybe it was another guy who looked like him."

"Yea, probably." He changed gears, "I'm sorry for your cousins, both him and his brother, their family, okay?"

"No, they're not okay. And they need help. I expect a small tribute, yes?"

"I'll look into it. Are we as François says, *pau*?"

"No. You'll get me a meet with all the principals. Pau isn't the answer." We stared at each other in the gloom of that rotten smelling bar, not a whole lot of affection between the two of us.

"I'll look into it." And he got up, pulling himself along the table with his fingertips to the edge so his ass wouldn't drag across the bench. A tired, strung out cocktail waitress of the rode hard, put away wet club asked me if I was done. I was but then I asked her if she were the regular daytime shift and if she knew the guy I had just been sitting with. She cocked her head.

"Mr. Fancy? Yea?" She said warily.

I pulled a sawbuck out of my wallet. "Yea?"

She looked at the fiver. "Mr. Fancy and the Big Spender." She shook her head, and started to turn.

"Hey, Mr. Jackson wants to know, okay?" She stopped and just turned her head to me. "Him I speak to. Abe ain't working as hard these days."

"The last time he was in?"

"With a big ass Hawaiian looking guy." She snatched the twenty out of my fingers."

"Want more? When?"

She looked at me as if I'd won the dumbass award. She gave me a lungful of cough before she spoke, " Like almost a week."

Banking on her reliability and not just hustling, it coincided with the DEA visit to Elihu's in Pacific Heights. This was not coincidence. I may have dropped Elihu's cheap Tokarev piece in Panama but that was only because I didn't want to use mine. Now I think I did.

Chapter 34

The ride from my mom and dad's to the airport area didn't take long at all. Their house overlooked the entire LA basin from near Loyola Marymount University. The best houses out here had been bought by the city and destroyed for the building of LAX but some areas still had clusters of houses in Westchester that had great views. This was one of those 'white flight' destinations. Those days. Everything had changed, demographically and geographically.

When did I throw the switch as a kid? When had I just turned off any and all empathy and cut my jets on morality? Had Sylvia brought things back for me, or was I pretending? My cousin was talking a blue streak; this Jewish guy she went to school with was already a doctor, this guy a lawyer, or some other had taken over the family business and living in Brentwood, Beverlywood, or Cheviot Hills. And because she so badly wanted to break out of her brunette ethnicity she married a blonde Jethro Bodine.

"Have a girlfriend, Remy?" She took me out of my little reverie.

"Yea, sort of." Not really wishing to talk about it, I felt it was a part of my private life; compartmentalized with all my other private lives.

"Thad and I were even swingers for awhile! Can you believe that? My mom would die on the spot if she knew. It happened at a party we went to in Ojai and we were both high. Yea, a Baptist who loved to smoke hash, can you believe it? Anyway, we ended up swapping with another couple after skinny-dipping and it was hot. So we did it a few more times." She was totally nonchalant about it.

"Really? I am surprised, Jen." I laughed. "Was that your lifestyle?" I wanted to tell her how Mickey Mouse that was compared to the Adult Disneyland of Magsaysay Street in Olongapo.

"It was okay until I got hit on by a black guy, and then all that old Kentucky boy erupted. It was fine as long as I was balling guys like him, but a black guy? No way, Jose. And that guy's wife was cute too."

"I can see that." I wanted to tell her about Sylvia, but kept my powder dry. I think she thought all this was shocking to me, or turning me on.

"How do you feel about that? Interracial stuff?"

"Doesn't bother me."

"Do you take quaaludes, Remy?" I hadn't, but I knew François handed them out to his girls when they were bored and they would get in the mood for work.

"Why? Have some?"

"Yea, want one?"

"Not while I'm driving! I've also been drinking."

"Silly, by the time it hits we'll be at the hotel bar. My treat."

I don't know why I did but I reached my hand out and she put a fat 714 in my palm. Like an idiot, I just mindlessly threw it down dry. Funerals have that power.

It was three a.m. when my eyes popped open and I had that feeling I used to have when sleeping in the bush if we weren't extracted by the ACM's or picked up by a Huey and tear-assing back to the relative safety of a ship or our hooches. I broke a sweat.

But I was only in a bed at the Holiday Inn, and next to me, one leg thrown over my thigh laid my cousin Jennifer. Oh son, I thought, your moral compass pushes due south and in the little dabs of memory I could see it all roll out. And I was still high; that trapped in the riptide fatigue weirdness that quaaludes gave you. My eyes were in alert mode, but the brains behind them just a warm fog, or a soaked sponge. My mouth tasted of vodka, cigarettes and for some reason talcum powder. Lying there I moved my head, back and forth in abject shame.

"Hmmm...Remy, are we in hell yet?" She slurred in a sleepy voice muffled by my neck, where her lips were walking.

I sighed, "Not yet, but definitely on the outskirts."

"Don't go all religious or guilty on me. Okay?"

"Doesn't make much sense to does it?" She slid down my chest taking blankets and anything else. She looked back up my chest in the dark.

"Good, cuz I'm not done."

I had no clue as to why it happened or why I let it. No doubt the combination of Nico's funeral, booze, depression and quaaludes helped. But all I had to do was raise my hand, and I didn't. Later, I pulled myself out of bed, and staggering to the shower just made it in. 'How feeling depraved am I?' After I was almost numb from the cold water stinging me, Jennifer came into the bathroom to squat, and then the curtain pulled back and she came in, screaming for the hot water.

"Don't look at me like that, Remy. It took two." She moved me over and holding her head back allowed the thick black hair to take the entire stream. She grabbed it like the mane of a fast horse and wringing it out, blew water off her lips, wiped her eyes and smiled. "Seriously, it was fun and I needed it. Who knew? We should've done this in high school."

So, with that we had moved from the outskirts to Hell Central. She handed me a washcloth and turned her ass to me. I had a memory of us on the side of La Cienega public pool in south Beverly Hills on a family swim outing when I toweled her off in 1960. Almost twenty years ago. Nick, Jack and I teasing her, whispering about her little 'buds' and catching Clovis smoking a cigarette outside near the tennis courts. Everyone was alive then. Young.

Later we smoked as she called room service for some bagels and coffee. I desperately wanted to call Sylvia and reconnect to her, hear her voice but knew even if I did she would just be getting off her shift and be dead tired. I decided to let it go and try and put a few hours between that time to talk, civilization, and this dog act.

"I did fuck that guy, the black guy, behind Thad's back. He would've killed us both had he known and as it was, in the entry way to our house, it was a wham-bam-thank-you ma'am because we were scared of Thad coming back sooner than anticipated." She was matter of fact, no big deal. "I could come visit you in San Francisco, Remy, if you liked." I thought I heard that voice of Mr. Johnson say Hello Satan, I believe its time to go.

I put out my cigarette." I have to go. I need to see my folks and fly home." I shrugged. "I don't even know what to say."

She smirked, "Don't say anything. Just leave it a good private memory. Just between us. When you want, when alone, you can open this little package of the past and think of me. Thad said one of the reasons he quit the swinging scene was because in his words I, 'turned men into pigs' and he had trouble dealing with it. Do you feel like a pig?"

" I'm not oinking, *yet*. Thinking this relationship isn't in the realm of normalcy or has a shelf life past today, Jen." I tried to make it light, but I sounded weak.

"Stop wrestling with morality or your karma. You act like you've been turned into a pig! You're not. Just the experience alone was hot for me." I leaned over and kissed the top of her head, fragrant from her shampoo. "Semper fi, Jen."

"Remy?" I stopped in the doorway, raising my eyebrows. "Did you kill anyone in the war?"

I left quietly and pulled the door shut, walking the passageway to the elevator surrounded by ghosts.

"What happened to you last night? We thought you were taking your cousin to the hotel and then coming back? I needed you to help people home, and to come with me when I took Constance to the home." He wasn't too happy.

Partial truth works, "Jen and I had some drinks, pop, and I guess my fatigue from Panama and the funeral just caught up to me. I stayed there."

He was incredulous, "In her room?"

"There were twin beds, pop. I just passed out. I'm sorry I didn't come back." He didn't know how sorry.

"Shit! Everything is shit. That family is decimated and crushed. Nico and Costas were their reasons for living. Nico…a beautiful boy. Was going to be successful too." My dad looked as bad as I did but for better reasons.

"He was engaged too." I said in a low voice.

"What? When did he tell you?"

"Before he left for Panama, we talked."

"Shit, he didn't tell anyone else. Does his fiancée even know?"

"I'm not sure. She might've called the house, maybe during the time after the funeral and talked to some family. If she didn't contact anyone then no." I thought of that broken arrow and it wasn't making me feel any better.

"Is she Greek?"

"Yea, she's Greek. I can't remember her last name though, her first name is Sofia."

My dad's hair is this mix of white and black, like it can't make up its mind to be grey. He ran his hands through it. He looked at me coldly.

"Tell me to my face, right here. Did you know or have any hand in any of this Remy?"

I looked him dead in the eyes and said very slowly, "No. I had no idea what Costas was doing or the people he was involved with." He put his hand on my shoulder, and with an appreciative smile gave it a squeeze like he used to after a little league game when I had a couple of hits.

I was that good of a liar.

Chapter 35

I called the operator later that morning to charge the long distance call to my home phone and left a brief message on Sylvia's machine. I pictured her asleep, drapes pulled tight against the day and her machine, in the living room of her flat taking my voice. I tried to make it sound normal but after a night of well vodka, cigarettes and little sleep, it sounded like a frog smoking a cigar.

I booked a mid evening flight so I could have a dinner with my mom and dad. I made a lot of small talk about the garage, my new position blah blah blah to keep their minds off the two brothers. It worked up until the point I was leaving and my mom broke down. She said every day I was in Viet Nam she cried and prayed for me. Looking at my dad over her shoulder as she hugged me, he looked uncomfortable.

"Did you pray for me too?" I asked him. I didn't even know why.

He gave me a 'phooey' with his hand and came up, pulling my mom off me.

Later, as I was about to shuffle out the door he came back to me. He had that furtive look that said this is between you and I and not your mother.

"Your mother was concerned you'd become a *fonias* there. I never asked you. Its something a man can't ask, especially his son. My father, rest his soul, knew I'd killed men in the infantry, so there was no questions. But it was a different war. We weren't called murderers by people or the press."

"War is war, Pop. People get killed, justly and wrongly."

"So you've made your peace?"

I laughed, "That's a back door 'did you kill anyone' question."

He shrugged, "After the war I had nightmares about combat. Your mother would be frightened by my waking up screaming."

"Really?" I stared at him. I had missed that part.

"Its why she prayed every night so cut her some slack. One day you'll have a wife and she'll know you've been to war."

"Would you care who I married? Who my wife would be?"

"What does that mean?"

"If my wife wasn't Greek, wasn't white?"

He shook his head as if id asked 'what if I married a tree.' "Why do you ask such silly questions?"

And that answered that. I slept the entire flight.

Back in the city I had a lot of things to do. This year for some reason seemed hotter, as if we'd been knocked off course and headed into the sun like Icarus, our wings melting and headed for doom. San Francisco wasn't even destined for a cool summer. This was different. Later on, before things changed, Sylvia and I swam at Baker's Beach it was so hot. I remember it because they'd just found the Italian PMs body in the trunk of a car. And that reminded me of Nick.

Chapter 36

Elihu fell by my place to get me and we jetted down Lincoln to 19th Avenue to head towards the bridge on a typical day; sun shining on Divisadero Street yet in the Sunset and Richmond, cool grey fog. I imagined Jack's flat in Noe Valley awash in sunlight with people walking in shirtsleeves and tanks. In Elihu's convertible I was shivering in an old red USMC sweatshirt, but all it took was thinking of the humidity of Panama and you'd hear no complaints of the cold. The embrace of the sun would slip off my tongue as easily as the lies I told Sylvia and my parents.

Once on the bridge, I just shut my eyes and had my head back. Elihu had jazz on the radio, Chet Baker to Marin County and some house out at Stinson Beach so I could have a sit down with the people who quite possibly had Jack's existence in their hands. Or extinction.

The house smelled of old money even from outside. This was no modern built place. Off the road down a steep driveway it was half hidden behind two twisted and windswept cypress trees that I imagined at night caught the wind, making a beautiful noise. I also bet the people who lived there didn't give a shit how the wind sounded; the house just being a chip needed to maintain the lifestyle. Elihu was one of those guys. As fine as his house on Filbert was it meant nothing to him. Neither did the Russian and Telegraph Hill houses nor the Russian River house in Sebastopol.

He wasn't coming in so as I got out he was shot gunning a dab of blow. I walked to his side of the car, leaned over; motioning to him I wanted a blast. I could taste it in the back of my throat, that medicinal numbing following it fast. I also took one of his expensive ridiculously fat cigarettes and lighting it, walked to the door.

It was a heavy carved oak affair affecting a giant spread of conifers with a body of water and sailboat in the distance not unlike a Japanese ran-mah. I knew once open, the inside of the door would reflect the outside like a mirror. I knocked.

A tall guy with a receding hairline of chestnut brown opened the door about a foot, looked at me and behind me at Elihu and then opened the door wider. He was in a polo shirt and slacks with a pull down shoulder holster moored to his belt and the butt of a 1911 staring at me.

"Come in Remy." And I went in.

I turned around as he shut the front door and validated what I had thought of the reverse motif. Not weathered like the outside it was a beautiful job of craftsmanship. Turning back the guy faced me, arms out in front with his palms up in a gesture of apology and also for me to imitate. I turned and saw an original Picabia to the side of the door over a small high boy. I raised my arms in the same manner and he started to pat me down. He was a pro and after a few seconds he motioned me towards a doorway into a room lined with cedar walls and a koa wood cabinet, its swirls almost three-dimensional. A voice I knew called my name. It was Corky.

"My buddy Remy. How are you?" He reached out a toned arm and his smooth hand swallowed mine up, "Drink?"

"Cognac."

"Remy VSOP, of course." He made a gesture of abundance and turned towards a bar also made of brilliant almost blonde koa. Turning I saw Spin, Moochie and two guys I didn't know. Both looked like Wells

Fargo loan officers. Corky turned with my drink and Spin clapped his hands a little too loud.

"Alright...so here we are." He motioned me to a chair that stood alone facing the front of them as if I were in an amphitheater. The guy who was strapped leaned in the doorway staring out the windows. "Your request, so talk to us, buddy. What it is?" This last sentence spoken in a fake Flip Wilson jive voice attempt at ethnicity.

I took a drag, and then said slowly, "I want assurances that Jack is safe, and stays safe. He understood the risks and prepped for the worst-case scenario. And here it is and exacerbated due to his brother's murder in Panama City. His family is living a double tragedy and as it is he's shouldering that as well as his confinement. So I want to know he'll be safe. I've talked to him and he understands. There are no problems from his end, and I've seen where they have him, and in my estimate there might be some people who couldn't handle it." I looked around the room, not settling on anybody in particular, but one of the suits moved a bit in his seat. Moochie started to speak, but I cut him off. "Yea, the DEA has been interested and that's to be expected. They took the line of least resistance following up on his communications and KAs. I couldn't clear his desk at work and he should've been smart to do it prior to departure but he didn't. And that's that? And what's become of the investigation? Nothing. Just a bolo. So I need to know he'll be okay and finally he comes home, when he farts it makes a nice healthy noise. A nice healthy non-return valve that hasn't been compromised." I tapped about a half inch of ash of my cigarette, and then took a slow controlled drag.

"So what do *we* need to do in your estimate?" Moochie finally got in.

"He needs a bigger shot than five-K. He needs a ten thousand foundation to get the judicial connections in step. Everything we've shoved into this black hole down there has been to create a pleasant climate, good faith and a show of solidarity. The wheels of justice have just started turning. Marianos has spelled it out and you guys know the deal. I'm sure he isn't a stranger to your answering machines. From there, I can handle. I want your word, that money down, and that can secure any hard feelings."

Spin asked with a bit of cynicism, "Hard feelings?"

I took a nice bite of my cognac, my namesake. My hand was steady and I felt strong, back on point, "Yes. I want to know why Justin was in Panama City when my cousin Nick was murdered. Can you clear that up for me, please, and let's not play fiddle fuck. He was there. He pulled a rabbit after I got there."

The two suits looked at each other as to where this was going, and had the hey, I didn't sign on for this part look. They were there for nothing but cash, they hadn't signed on for this intrigue. Moochie looked at Skip who stared at me. I could barely see the strapped guy in the glare of the window, his reflection almost ethereal. I was sure he was staring at a point in the back of my head and remembering it. Corky coughed and smiled.

"Damn, once recon, always recon. He was there in case we needed him, no more no less."

"And did you need him? Need him to brace Nick because the DEA were trying to get their hooks into him and perhaps it was thought that the Weasel went south?" I took a swallow, still steady but only I knew I wasn't.

"What're you saying Remy?" Corky had lost his K-Mart greeter kindness.

"Answer my question." I could hear the unsnapping of the holstered piece from behind me. I didn't move.

Staring back at me, "He was there in case we needed him, no more no less. He saw he didn't need to stay so he left and he was in no way directed by us to involve himself in any action unless specified. In regards to Arthur…we had some doubts and still do, but he's gone to ground and lives there half the fucking time so he knows how to be invisible. The unfortunate…" And here he tried to find the word, "*coincidence* of Jack's brother's being taken off was horribly tragic. We know everything the DEA talked to him about because smartly, Nick told Marainos."

I felt like I had the high ground still, and pressed it. I pointed to the two guys on the couch, "And you fellows are…investors?"

I caught them off guard. Corky said, back in his hail good fellow voice, "Hey, Remy, these are friends we asked to sit in, they're not part of the conversation."

Lawyers! They would press these guys afterwards about legal footing plying them with blow, Raider's tickets, and chicks at Francois' houses—anything to keep their hooks in them if they weren't already being blackmailed already. I looked at Corky and smiled, giving him a wink. I was just sort of fucking off, sort of.

"So," I took a final swallow, "can I get those assurances? If you need me to run down there again I will. I wish you all had me running there after he was dropped. And his brother would be fucking his fiancée right now." I said this right to Corky, very casually. "So, agreed?"

The other two looked at Corky, who looked at his watch, looked out the window then back at the other two.

"Agreed." He answered without any discernable tone to figure out where he was coming from. He turned to the suits, "Pay him. Now."

I stood and walked to him, extending my hand. He looked at it with almost visible repulsion but slowly took it with a milquetoast shake that almost made me laugh out loud, and he disengaged just as quickly. He looked at the two suits and they stood up straightening their fat ties and throwing their arms, shooting their cuffs. Then they almost hit each other's heads bending over to get a briefcase. Corky shut his eyes, shaking his head in disgust.

It was a tad awkward now and I just needed to leave smartly, with the cash, under control. As I moved to leave this seaside room, Spin caught me, touching my shoulder with light fingers.

"Remy, did a little bird named Arthur tell you about Justin?" He employed the same neutral tone Corky used.

I turned, squared my shoulders, took a step closer to him, knowing he didn't like it and made him back off, smiling said no. Didn't he realize I'd threatened to kill the Weasel after the last run I took? Why would he approach, of all people, me? I said I saw Justin, him and his hillbilly wife at the Sheraton. Then I turned away and kept walking, admiring this woodwork inside the house. The strapped guys eyes following me. I encountered Corky one last time, as he was talking to Elihu when I got outside.

"Nice house, " I stretched then pulling the sweatshirt out of the car. "Must be nice to have friends like this."

He curled his lips and looked at the house, "Yea, it's a nice house. Built in like 1946 I think, yea Elihu? But it's too windy here for me. Even with the privacy. If you want to know more about it, just ask the owner."

I looked at Elihu, "You're the fucking owner."

"Told you to stop underestimating this guy Eli." He smacked the door top of the car and walked away.

I looked at Fuqua, "Really?" He looked away. I poked the back of his head. "You told them I was packing when I went to Panama didn't you?" That's why Justin did the high aqua out of there."

I didn't talk to him the entire way back to the city. I just thought about that house, and if I owned it I'd actually live in it.

Chapter 37

"Remy, what're you reading about?" Collier, one of the college guys asked me. He must have seen the intent on my face with the Chronicle in front of me.

"They just sentenced that crazy ratfucker Berkowitz 25 years to life for those Son of Sam shootings." I shook my head, "What a freak!"

Collier agreed, "I have a cousin in Queens who died her hair red 'cuz he wasn't hunting gingers, he was targeting brunettes."

"You don't say?" Then he was staring at me strangely. "What?"

"You sounded just like Dominic when you said that." And he went out of the office.

That was enough creepiness for me. Dominic. Since his funeral my overlords had been doing quick time with some deliveries and also I was sitting on a huge inordinate amount of cash. I felt like Horton, sitting atop this huge egg of laundered, filthy lucre. I knew better to even think about what the deal was, and that was fine with them. Every few days someone would fall by, we'd lock the office door and boom, into the safe another bag, or lets take one out. Luckily we had one of those old Mosler floor safes that could probably hold three or four bodies in it. We used to kid that they built the Pan-American around it. So that intrigue was going on.

The deal with Jack had rolled into a pattern. After my sit down with the Board and the suits, the situation was front-loaded and Sr. Marianos was running it as smooth as a Swiss watch. He not only had an in with the judge on Jack's case, he was sleeping with the judge's clerk and was privy to any and all of the moves being made. I received some mail from Jack, and I could tell by how chatty and fluid his letters were, that he felt secure. I had sent a case of books; comix, cards, board games and some porn to Marainos and Jack received it intact. It were as if the Gods were tired of who they first drove mad that they wished to destroy later and just took a day to go surf. Even Mickey Rat has a good day.

Sylvia had warmed to the idea of being closer to the USF Med Center, and we slowly and surely started moving her in. We didn't push it hard and we'd made up our minds just to treat it like jazz; one day a well composed piece, the next total freelancing. I liked her there. I felt normal. Or what I thought was normal. I moved my Sherlock stash of private stock to a different, secure location and my Colt was still safe under the bed on two pegs on the inner wood frame; one tit held the trigger guard and the barrel rested on the second. Life had taken on a mild pace.

Since conferring with Elihu at the bar and discovering he met Francois there so soon before me was a nut I hadn't cracked yet. It could've been anything. But that and Elihu's faux pas in regards to Justin's whereabouts when Nick was murdered and the fact he turned around and told the Disney boys I was packing regardless of who I was hunting, in their eyes the Weasel, but perhaps in Elihu's eyes Justin, also was a red flag for me.

I stayed away from Elihu's house in Pacific Heights since the drive to Stinson Beach and parlay with the powers that be. He was acting more aloof than usual, and when in contact, Mona would get me thinking about her; under my skin and silently spreading inside me. That last tidbit about her working in Saigon was a puzzle piece. I put the fact that I could balance her in my mind while involved with Sylvia to my basic flaw; I allowed the wrong things to happen.

Since visiting Francois' house in North Beach, he seemed unavailable even for a roadhouse beer. I did talk to him about the World Cup, but it was just odds and money. I did have one kindred spirit in the whole drama that centered on Jack:

The Weasel.

Politics and dope make strange bedfellows.

Doc Krinberg

Chapter 38

We'd been snuggling, some thirty minutes after lovemaking and the sweat from the intensity had finally dried. It had been that good, that beautiful. I was almost gone when I heard my ancient and noisy doorknob turning slowly and the slick of a plastic card leaving the lock. I was rolling quickly and with one hand under the bed frame to take the .45 off its tits, assuming the position as if I were on the range, half hidden by my old armoire. The knob of the bedroom door turned ever so slightly and it opened towards me, affording me more cover behind it so my rush would be hidden unless I tripped and blew it.

The long ugly black snout of a silencer emerged. I hit the door hard catching his extended arm hard and pulling it back quickly, repeated it hearing the owner unleash a scream and a guttural curse. The weapon dropped. Sylvia, behind me to my left was sitting up in bed. I turned and violently jerked my head over to the closet, making her go there. She sprung up and ran inside as I was around the door already and caught Justin as he was trying to get his backup piece out of an ankle holster with his left hand. I brought the butt of my gun down on his melon, and then whipped his face with the muzzle at high speed. He tapped out after that move, and standing nude I figured this was a good time to put on pants and take care of Sylvia.

I secured his weapons and knew I had some explaining to do. And it wouldn't be fun. I went to the turntable; 'Let it Bleed' was sitting there so I started it, and turned the volume up. I came to the door she was peeking out of, and jumping out hugged me and asked what the hell? Who is this guy? Lets call the cops! She was shaking in fear. I had to get back and secure Justin's hands and feet, sequester him in the front room with her in the bedroom. I swooped to the closet and grabbing a kimono gave it to her, and pulling the other from the closet I took the sash and went back to him, still nude, and tied him like a hog. I held his primary piece, the silenced .380 and his back up, a hammerless .38 I threw on the bed, finally pulling a pair of Levi's on. Returning to Sylvia I tried to calm her as best as possible, and told her I couldn't call the cops and asked her just to stay in the bedroom as I needed to ask this guy some questions, please. She looked at his bleeding face and went into nurse mode.

"No!" I grabbed her. "No medical attention, stay in the bedroom!" And then dragging him out over the threshold I shut the door behind me. He popped open one eye, shaking the blood out of it and found a position he could live with. I looked at him, aiming his own gun at his midsection.

"Tell it, pogue. Tell it. Why and who sent you?" I was coming down after the initial contact with him.

"Up yours," he spat on my wood floor, blood running into his mouth from where I'd whipped his face, using the front sight to bust his upper lip.

"The Boys send you? Or maybe someone else?" I shifted the .380 and wiped my right hand on my pants.

"Nothing to say…you're not calling the cops and you wont kill me. You've got your tar baby stashed in there and wont do shit while she's here." He laughed and spat more out.

"I just missed you in Panama, bitch. Someone told you to get on your horsey and ride. Who?"

He just grinned, shaking his head. Then he yelled loudly, "Hey, Tar baby! I've met your roommate, the hag with the wigs?" I gave [a] smack on the cheek; he hung his head moaning, not quite passed.

Sylvia emerged from the bedroom shaking, holding the kimono tight around her as if it were snowing in the room. "What did he say? Why has he been to *my* flat? Who in the hell is he Remy?"

Justin started laughing, spitting again, "I'm your nightmare, tar baby and your mudshark boyfriend can't save you. He couldn't save his pussy cousin either."

"SHUT UP!" I went into the bedroom and getting a pillowcase came back and pulled it over his head, hitting the top of the case hard, Justin moaning.

"Remy...tell me, what is this all about? Is this about your cousin in jail? This guy knows you, knows where I live? Is he part of all that down south? The dope deal? Tell me, baby" She was shaking.

I put my fingers against my temples, I had to figure this out, put it together. I turned to her, "He works for the guys Jack went south for—and he has it in his mind that I'm in need of disappearing for whatever reasons. I made some demands on these guys to take care of Jack. He's probably been watching me and that's how he knows you, as a known associate of mine. It's the only things I can think of." Jesus, it all sounded like bullshit even as the words left my mouth.

" A known *associate*? What are you going to do to him? Lets call the police and have him arrested. He came here to kill you...us!" She looked at the table where my .45 rested as her fear now turned to mixed anger. "Is that *your* gun? I didn't know you had a gun?"

"I don't know what to do with him, but not the police. That would be a bad idea."

"You just can't *shoot* him?" She looked at me incredulously. I don't even know what expression I was wearing but it scared her.

Justin must've been working his hands slowly as we talked to each other. I wasn't paying attention, more concerned about Sylvia. He had the hood off and was with one hand, getting at my gun arm before I knew what the fuck. His feet were still tied so it was awkward but caught me off guard. The gun squibbed out of my hand and Sylvia thinking quickly stooped and grabbed it. He started quick punching me with his free hand

"Give me that gun, nigger or your ass is going to be sorry your coal burning fucking boyfriend ever breathed." I exploded at that and grabbing his wrists jerked him up and head butted him hard, he slackened in my grip, I lost it then.

"The fuck did you call her? You piece of shit walk the dog piss in the sink wash your balls in a cup fucking white trash motherfucker? You need to be thinking of your little hillbilly cunt right now and your life insurance, you Jody fuck." I stomped on his balls, getting a huge 'ooomph' out of him, and then I was reset for a follow up.

"Remy! Stop! You'll kill him!" She pleaded. I turned to her.

"The fuck do you think he was doing here? He's not here to talk," I pointed at the silenced auto in her hands, taking it from her. "He's a fucking life taker. He's here to clip me, and in the bargain clip you too."

"Are you involved in that coke smuggling?"

Wheezing, Justin croaked out, "Yes, you fucking dumb cooze, up to his fucking eyeballs…he's a goddamn…" I stomped on his balls again, and still holding onto his arm, twisted it. This shut him up. I retied his hands this time until they were white, and then started going thru his pockets.

His wallet was filled with the usual crap and a picture of a pasty blonde with a bad shag cut and a fat, toothless, melon headed baby. He also had about $500 in mixed 50's and 20's. I pulled the pic, money and his driver's license.

His shirt pocket had a folded paper stating:

The Winter Spider

Karras—617 Hugo, garret, Pan-American Garage, Pine
Jones—USF Med Center, 1908 Steiner Street, back door lock weak

I turned the record over, and Sylvia had returned to the bedroom but the door was still ajar. Out of the corner of my eye she was on the bed, one leg under her. I leaned down and grabbed him by the hair, shaking him.

"Listen, asshole, and take a good look," I showed him the snapshot of his family." If you have any feelings for them, you're going to talk. Or they're going to get a visit like this and you wont be there to do shit about it."

He laughed, but I could tell it was hurting him, "Fuck you. They're not even there, man. Tough guy, tough marine…you wouldn't have the stones for it. Like your fucking cousin…promised he wouldn't help the DEA and begged…just wanted to live his life, like a pussy." I grabbed him by the throat.

"He was a citizen you asshole, he wouldn't have hurt anyone…who told you to brace him?" At the mention of Nico I had this enormous rush of guilt, like when you're about to throw up, but there was also anger of white heat and I felt as if I were ripping out of my skin.

"So what?" He spat blood at me again, "And you and this nigger are as good as fucking worm meat, nothing's going to stop that, so untie me asshole." He turned his head, "Hey, Tarbaby…get your black ass out here…" I didn't let him finish.

Sylvia rushed out of the bedroom…in my head someone said it was *just a shot away.* After I pulled the case back over his face, I put my left thumb into an eye like he was a bowling ball, Even above the music we could hear him as I applied pressure; this high whining scream of sheer pain, and I pushed it in even deeper...*rape, murder*...I knew there was a round jacked up in the chamber and with just fluid action, his scream and Sylvia's NO! I pushed the muzzle of the silencer into the space of the other eye. The discharge threw a flame over the cream-colored case and powder burns appeared in a huge star pattern and his head would've jerked clean away had I not my thumb buried in his right eye. The shell ejected, flew to the right, landing on my hearth, under the Gauguin, the slide jacking in another round that I sent to follow its brother into the blackened hole in the material. The case burned momentarily and settling, the area I was in was full of a small, dissipating fog; gun smoke and blood mist. Cordite and burned flesh was stark and like pepper in the air. I heard...*it's just a kiss away.*

Then I came out of it, I stood still holding the gun, letting go of Justin's remaining eye under the case, smoke still seeping from the case and the end of the silencer. I walked into the bedroom and Sylvia moved away from me, as if I were a huge slow moving snake slithering by. From the other room...*All my love's, in vain*...I went to the phone and called the number the Weasel had given me for this one Bay Area safe house. I turned the music down and after calling once, hanging up, calling again he answered.

"Wh-wh-what's up?" I almost passed out from the relief of hearing he was actually up here.

"Justin paid a visit."

"That's p-past tense. And?"

"I need a suit pressed." This was a euphemism for needing a cleaner. "But I need time. I'll leave a key under the mat."

"Okay, on my way." He hung up. Sylvia just stared at me.

"Lets get dressed. We need to get out of here for now." She said nothing, just automatically started gathering gear for the bike. I threw an

The Winter Spider

old serape I had over the figure on the floor. He was in that careless attitude of a laundry bag just dropped there. I also got a towel and said a silent thank you his head rested on the hardwood floor, and there wasn't an excess of blood, maybe indicating hollow points. My face hurt where he'd hit me and I realized I had trouble moving it from a fist I took to the neck when he got free. I went straight to the bedroom and found my Sherlock stash in the compartment under the window seat and tapped out a couple mounds on the back of my hand, scoffed those up and then rubbed a little on the side of my face and neck. I just went thru the motions on auto, and then lit a cigarette. Looking up I saw the shock and disgust on Sylvia's face. I came out of my trance quickly then.

"Not believing what I'm seeing...and who was that you called? Who are you, Remy? You're not even shaking," was all she said, standing there dressed, holding her shoulder bag, eyes looking dead tired. A little voice in my head said to no one; but I saved us.

I went into the bedroom, on automatic, finished dressing, and locking the flat, and putting the key under the mat we went down to the bike. I left his two guns in the flat and strapped mine up in its holster. The only place I could think of was our respite at Half Moon Bay. The entire ride down she held the bottom of the seat, avoiding any contact with me if possible.

Chapter 39

We got down there after 2 a.m. but the night clerk had a room that overlooked the beach. It was warmer down here than in the City but the ride down had been damp and cold. We said nothing, just moved as if lost within our own worlds. Inside the room we were trapped together. The bed filled the middle, and we stood on opposites sides of it, the shiny blue of the spread our ocean. I was on the window side, so I pulled the chair over to the sliding door and the lanai, cracked it open and smoked. I wasn't even trying to process what had happened. I'd relived it over and over as we drove down PCH. I could hear her sit on the bed behind me.

She started speaking, but her voice was in this disembodied place and it was like she wasn't even in the room.

"I was sitting there in your flat while you were at work and it was a hot day so I cracked the window, just as you have now so I could smoke. Remember that silk cocoon, the one wedged against the frame and window? Out of nowhere I heard this disgusting high-pitched whirring buzzing noise, going over to it I looked up. That thing had emerged and in its palps and fangs a blue bottle fly was trapped. That thing had come out hungry and crazy and if there were anyway to describe what that poor fly was doing I would say it was screaming. It were as if every evil laying dormant, every bit of hunger, madness and inchoate need exploded out of that cocoon and was unleashed on that poor fly. And when he, whoever that guy…that disgusting little disease carrier who came to your rooms and was in your clutches it were as if I was watching it again. I've never seen so much anger and white-hot violence. And yet here you are, a couple of bumps of cocaine and you're as cool as the city in November. No flies on you—ready to face the day no matter you just killed someone who's a part of a criminal network *you* belong to.

"I'm a nurse, Remy, with a crazy ass mother following a religious fanatic to South America, who according to what little info I could glean has gone off the rails and conducts suicide drills. This is my reality, and the main thing, the glue keeping me together; keeping me from tripping is my career and you. *You* Remy. My love for you, and my idea of a future with you to build up something special and good…but you're a garden-variety hood. You're a 'seventies cliché like disco, the big drug gangster. God, why?"

And she just cried. I didn't even try to explain it. It would've sounded bogus from Jump Street. Just folly.

I must have smoked five or six cigarettes sitting there, as if I were falling endlessly thru the clouds praying to hit bottom. But, so far, so good. She pulled up the desk chair and sat next to me.

"I don't think I want to be around you when you lose control of that darker side you have; the anger that you shelter. There's no mercy that can help you, Remy. You know that don't you? You'll just keep spinning like some lifeless thing in space. Just turning in your anger, destroying everything in your little orbit. You would destroy me too." She looked away, out the window to sea. I started feeling numbed, as if I were freezing by inches, degrees at a time.

She couldn't bring herself to look me in the eyes, as if any and all answers she sought were out there in the blackness over the dead grey sea.

"We used to come here on the bike and I felt it was our place; sanity maintenance. I used to revel in just sitting behind you feeling your body as we rode. But now I feel like a refugee. And I'm lost. I'm trying to find a place inside me that's still feels safe with you and I can't." She looked up and as she did a tear fell over the rim and darkened her cheek. I was empty inside watching it. I'd been the author of it; sole possession was mine. I could physically feel the moorings between us snapping and breaking, I dared not even touch her. I knew if my hand so much as brushed against her she would be repulsed as if no less than that thing in the silk cave had walked over her skin. She turned to me quickly.

"Did you play me since day one? Did you have this secret life, walking next to you, like your shadow? Its there with you always—at work, when you're out with me, when we're in bed," her voice got flat, " Like some creepy stranger, peeping me when I have no inhibitions and vulnerable. It's as if I am fucking two men at the same time and I don't know which is the real man. And cocaine too-boot?!" Her tears just rolled now, sometimes into the tracks of previous tears, others finding dry skin to penetrate. "You knew or were a part of Jack's trip since the beginning—while we were together. That day at Joe's when you told me about it and I told you I loved you…you just shit on all of that Remy." She used her sleeve to wipe her nose.

"Sylvia..." She slapped me so hard I thought I'd taken a round to the face.

"I'm a nurse. A nurse. I deal with life, sustaining it, nurturing it, fixing it, maintaining it and sometimes losing it. Like you've lost me."

She got up, and after shutting the bathroom door I could hear the lock being turned. Then I rode home alone.

Doc Krinberg

Chapter 40

"How do you move around without these guys knowing it?" It were as if the Weasel were part Houdini and Chandu.

He picked something out of his teeth, "I've free-lanced, and lived abroad and t-traveled so much they c-can't know everything I do. They're not as omniscient as they make out and Elihu plays that b-bullshit up a lot. By the way, how is that p-poseur?"

"The same but more nervous since all this shit has gone down with Jack, all the parts moving in that scene."

"No doubt. He was always a p-pompous eunich."

"They're still looking for you, on one level or the other. They're convinced you fingered Jack, you were compromised and that turned you into a *grass*, and that's from a report from whomever they had down there...and I'd like to know whom it was. Justin again? Has your status changed?"

He had this wry little smile, "Well, lets say they're looking at several options, one being it m-might not be me."

"Like me? Is that why they tried to clip me and Sylvia?"

"*If* that was their idea to begin with you have to wonder where they got it from? And who p-put in the word. Who's the most threatened by you?" He took out a cigarette. "I know you asked yourself a question when you saw Francois' house in North B-Beach. I mean, c'mon...that b-big fucking moke in Little Italy?" I had asked François the same thing but he said he couldn't answer those questions yet.

We were eating at a place in the east bay at around midnight. I had called in sick and we spent the day cleaning. I also got a blast from the guy who lived in the 2nd floor flat about cranking the Stones up so loud when he was in a dead sleep. Apologizing, I assured him I would never again. The Weasel talked to me with his head turned, looking to the side, or behind us. We all sort of did that as if we were expecting death or the cops to stroll in. We were trying to cut thru a piece of leather they'd advertised as steak and eggs.

"When I was setting up the first run, we had the incident of the first m-mule, and I thought I smelled a rat. The g-guy was stand up, no marks against him. He didn't even use for fuck's sake. He liked his drink. But then b-boom! He was dead. Od'ed. He was a family friend of Spin's—that's how close he was to the D-boys. No trust issues. He was even fucking one of Francois' g-girls and no reports from there of silly behavior. This is when the bottom fell out and they needed someone to use as a damage c-control plug. Jack stepped up."

I just shook my head, trying to pull the edges of the story, enlarge it, and expand it so I could see beyond. I felt like one of those morons on The Price is Right over guessing the cash value while everyone in the audience groans.

"Then," he continued, " I get a t-telegram to call San Francisco, call Elihu. So I did."

"And? Was this early spring?

"Indeed it was." This would place it around the time Elihu wanted to bail—due to the Weasel's disappearance. "Said to take a t-two week vacation, that *you* were t-tracking me, already in country," he almost laughed saying it, "He said don't tell the D-boys, or François—just

The Winter Spider

submerge and p-pop up in two weeks. Don't call anyone, don't write, just beat feet."

"And just like that, you took off. Where'd you go?"

"Montivideo. I'd always wanted to go there, and that's that. I did get a c-couple of messages at the main store we import from for the wives outlet in Berkeley, and there was also a message from Mona telling me the c-coast is c-clear, you'd returned to the city. I didn't return the c-calls from the store because I thought you might be tracking me thru the businesses."

"Didn't you explain anything to the Boys? Up here everyone got paranoid when you vanished. And fucking Mona knew I was in town, never leaving. Man, she knows where her bread is buttered."

"If she *even* knew what was going on. Of course they d-did. But Elihu told me to just say I had a business deal to c-contend with, job related."

"I never left the city, and Elihu explained to me that you'd simply taken a bolt, no words exchanged, and people were upset. He actually tried to get me to exchange my funds for his so he could walk clean. Anybody else talk to you during that period?" I was curious. I think I knew who had. Arthur smiled his weasely best.

"Who do you think?"

"Francois." He said 'bingo' as he gave me the gunman's salute, winking.

It started to take shape like a sunbeam coming thru a window when you blew smoke on it revealing its geometric design as it swirled around it. Francois and Elihu started to come into focus, hard.

We were driving north east now, and he crouched over the wheel with a furtive look on his face. "Remy…I realized after that run down there with you I had a p-problem that I knew it was wrong but at the same time I didn't, you know? Anyway, I went to a d-doctor after that trip. I knew the girls were too young. I felt like fucking P-Peter Lorre in 'M'..."

I didn't know what to say, I just nodded yes in the dark.

"So thanks for that, okay?"

"Okay." I remembered the disgust I felt when I went into his room thru the adjoining door of the suite and saw him and the two girls; all three ripped on blow and booze. They were undressed with the exception of their panties, firm hard small tits poking out framed by thick long brown hair. In the center sat Arthur, nude with exception of his fucking porkpie hat and beach sox. It was just this repulsive tableau to walk in on and he saw the utter horror on my face, probably the same Sylvia had for me, and he offered one of them to me.

"Remy...take C-Concha. C'mon man, p-p-p-party." Concha, in her coke jittery way started peeling her panties down looked like a slinky going down the stairs trying to take its clothes off she was buzzing so hard I swore I could hear it like live tension wires. This blow was uncut and dangerously potent. I just took a beer from his reefer and backed out of the room, shutting the door and swearing I'd kill him if he ever brought it up. The last vision I had was of a pubescent Concha falling over, panties around her knees.

The memory gave me a shiver, but I took him at his word. Right now I needed him. Maybe not tomorrow, but today he had a white hat. He was looking at me to grab a clue as to where it was at so I smiled, said 'fuck you' laughing and lit a cigarette. He took that as the 'all clear' and probably held me in the same place I held him; alive today, wary eye to the future.

"Do you have another piece?" I asked. "If you need one I have his hammerless thirty-eight. Nice weapon." The .380 would go the grave with its owner.

"No. I'm g-g-good. Besides, who knows what p-p-peccadilloes that p-p-piece has p-p-performed and some c-cold case hounds are waiting to hear from it again to match ballistics to some c-croaking somewhere."

The Weasel had helped me clean, and he was quite adept, earlier after I returned from Half Moon Bay in regards to Justin's unfortunate series of events. He arrived in a '65 Ford Country Squire station wagon that we placed the body in after eleven at night, and drove east across the bridge towards Oakland. We were headed to an area near the Naval Weapons Station in Benicia, which was a good swampy area; marshlands on the inter-land water way. I thought it was a bit far and a little dangerous driving around with a cut up stiff in the back, wrapped in three shower curtains and duct taped but after we stopped to eat got the feeling this wasn't his first trip out here. I guessed right.

We pulled up to an area off a side road he seemed familiar with, got out of the car; an expanse of darkened marshes in front of us as the frogs, toads and crickets quieted at our presence. The tide was up, so the funk was minimal.

"Remember Ch-Chappy?" He asked, staring out at the horizon, the lights of the Naval Station in the distance.

"Yea. Elihu's buddy who ran that furniture restoration place next to Doggy Diner in the Mission."

"Same." He poked his chin out towards the marsh. "Say hello to him."

Chappy had been a hanger on, a guy who liked his recreational drugs and made a lot of money at his shop what with the gentrification going on in the older neighborhoods. He'd just be a random guy who turned up on the radar to cop some blow once in awhile. And then he was gone. At Arthur's words, I found myself giving a little beauty pageant wave towards the water, and then caught myself. And I didn't want to hear the story, the reason. History.

It was a slog and was glad I had on *boro-boroz* clothes I could just trash when finally home. The ride back was quiet and creepy. I started adding it all up. Elihu and François. The diversion to cast a shadow on the Weasel and the sudden death early in the game of the first mule, who coincidentally was with one of Francois' girls who might've slipped him a hotshot. It was as if they were trying to shitcan the entire run but then up popped Jack. Jack the lad, ready to jump in and save the day. And then boom, he's down. No keys, no pay-off. Just pissed off people, with exception of those two. But why?

Arthur spoke up. "Ever ask yourself who really sent Justin down to P-Panama City? Was it really the D-boys or someone else under the auspices of a concerned citizen, who convinced the Boys to send him…as a second set of eyes? And then tell him what he was told to say? That I supposedly gave a 'signal?'"

"I figured the Boys just sent him and at the meet they pretty much took responsibility for his being there."

"Of course they would. Those guys would never admit taking Elihu's advice. Or ever get their hands d-dirty." I was starting to be a believer in the dead mule on the toilet seat story about him. "So I'm thinking Eli and François."

"They can barely stand each other. To Eli that pineapple is the *untermenschen*."

"Who better to c-control? Strange bedfellows, man. Money and whatever else they got going on."

"Tell me about Jack. Did he fuck anything up? Or was he standup?"

"He was g-good. He's a little arrogant and in the hotel thought he was James Bond with the wine list, but he was all right. Talked about c-cars, which ones sell, etc. He doesn't get you, but then again, you're an enigma…even to the D-Disney's. I think they're frightened of you like they are of Francois, but in a different way."

I shook my head, "What doesn't he get? Because I pull down a union job, date interracially…that's his issue, not mine."

"I think its because you d-don't aspire to be a junior mafia member, or live in Noe. He did okay. It was when we got b-bottle necked in Panama and slightly separated. He had this big ass b-boombox and they were on his back like a short overcoat. He didn't have Buckley's chance of getting thru. I left the airport after modifying my ticket and then c-called Marainos. Then a c-coded call to the shop in Berkeley that was of course relayed to Corky." He laughed, " 'I sing the b-body electric'—-my signal to the Boys that the toilet was flushed and maybe with the right babying a street value of close to $550,000. You know what the price of a gram is now, and that its been stepped on G-God knows how many times and with what, you can q-quadruple your money and if its mob shit and they used talc or b-baking soda, or crystalized horse p-piss even, its all shit. I wouldn't go near it but your yuppies in Mendocino and the Marina, Alamo Square and Twin P-Peaks are clueless."

Then a loud bell went off in my head. I was doing some accounting work with Mr. Peabody the 2nd, and making sure our books reflected tickets and invoices for the monthly renters when one of the suits dropped in. It wasn't Matranga but a big bald guy with a banana nose and a circus strong man mustache. Jack had been in a month and a half and after the accountant excused himself, this gorilla, Polli, asked how things were. I said just peachy, life was good, the whole nine yards. Then out of nowhere he asked if any of the crew used dope, specifically coke. I knew the part time college guys smoked pot on the roof before they went home at night, but also pretty sure no one used shit, with the exception of me. I asked why and he said it was dry, the street prices would be rocketing and we should beware that theft would become a concern. I thanked him and then dismissed it. He gave me a pat on the back. I handed him his envelope and he left smiling.

That whole sequence played in my head. Mob controlled dope doubled, maybe tripled. The D-boys and their ilk didn't get their massive payday and four keys that could've stretched into summer was DOA. Francois opens a house in North Beach, Little Italy and I was pretty sure city documents on microfiche of recorded escrows would tell me what name owned the property but I already knew that. It would either be Elihu's mother if not his own. It all just made sense and also made me very tired. The two of them meeting to get their line of shit straight, tighten stories and maybe that's when they decided to whack me. Have Justin visit me, the loose cannon. I knew it wasn't the D-boys. They wouldn't be as dramatic as having me hit in my own flat. They'd invite me somewhere desolate with some lie about a meet, a BBQ or a pickup, whack me out in a secure place and then dump me out there. And how did they know about Sylvia? Elihu and Francois knew.

"Elihu and Francois rigged the whole thing. They snitched out Jack, put Justin on Nick…and they may have wished to just scare him but somehow that went wrong. They've been blowing smoke up the D-boys' ass. It all makes sense."

He shook his head, "I'm sort of c-coming to that same place. Action?"

I laughed, "Wow. It's a fucking bold move to be sure. Fortune Favors the Bold, until you fuck up. I'm going to just grab a few things from my flat and go under. I have to. How long will you be at that number you gave me?"

"Tomorrow, then I move to another location. I'll be c-closer in, out by SF State."

"I'll be moving tomorrow to Noe, Jack's flat for a couple of days." I sighed, exhausted. "Can you drop me at Irving and 7th? I need to cut thru the yards and get up to my flat from the backside."

"No problem." Me and the Weasel. Batman and Robin. What the fuck else could happen?

Chapter 41

My flat was dead quiet. Outside I could hear the light murmur of traffic. I walked over to the place where Justin had settled and it was spotless with a faint odor of cleaning agent still lingering. The Weasel just had a lot of things in his bag of tricks. A jack-of-all-trades. And I was duly thankful. I didn't want to go into the bedroom. I relaxed in the front room and smoked. I put on Klemmer's 'Touch' and decompressed. She and I had made love to that a lot. I fell asleep.

The phone woke me.

I had Polli, one pissed off Italian in my ear asking me where in the fuck I was.

"I'm in my flat, you called me," I mumbled not even thinking.

"I fucking know that, Karras, you're supposed to be *here*. I'm waiting to get into the safe. Are you still sick?" Now I busted a sweat. I'd forgotten these guys in all the other piles of shit I'd been stepping in.

"I'll be down there in a bit, sorry. Still didn't feel good." Putting on my servitude voice as well as possible. I could picture him shaking in anger, trying to maintain his temper. "Listen, go next door to the Arab's place and have a coffee, a Danish and tell him, his name is Khalid, to put it on my charge."

Then I pulled a hooker shower in the sink, shaved with cold water and praising the Great Green Frog, thankful I had my bike.

After this morning fiasco I needed to square myself away. My life's footlocker was in disarray. I couldn't tell Mr. Made Man, hey, I was busy ditching a stiff I'd clipped in my flat out near a federal weapons station with a walking felony called the Weasel.

I took care of him, was told not to fuck up, and when I went next door to see Khalid and take care of him I learned my sharkskin-suited buddy had charged three cartons of cigarettes besides breakfast. That made me laugh.

Nothing else happened that day. I hid in the office pretty much catching a few power naps. During one I dreamed I was with Sylvia.

"Remy?"

I awoke to Calloway at the door. "Ready?"

I took my feet off the desk, lit another cigarette and nodded 'yes.'

"Man, you look like shit!" He laughed.

'Thanks, you should see the other guy." I got up; changed out of my garage uniform and I started to think about killing Justin. Whoever sent him, never heard from him again. That would start somebody sweating somewhere. But is it the people I think it is? Thinking it could be Francois sort of hurt. We had the bond of the Corps. Elihu? Just a rich shitbird. Justin's old lady would have an emergency out I figured. Money stash, a safe house to run too, or a ticket back to Assgrab, Kentucky. She might have a number to call too, and wondered if she made that call. And if she did, did it induce a freakout? I had his license and home address. Walnut Grove. I wondered if it were real.

I looked at his keys and figured if his damn car was in the neighborhood, it was time to get rid of it. I hoped he parked close to the house and not way the fuck over near Golden Gate Park or in the Haight and walked into the neighborhood.

The Winter Spider

I strolled around and recognized a few of the V-dubs I knew resided here. Near Lincoln and 5th Avenue was a powder blue hatchback, probably a '72. There was a ticket on the windshield held fast by a wiper blade. I casually went to it and trying the passenger side lock the key rotated and it unlocked. Looking up and down the street I leaned inside and looked it over before going to the driver's side. In the backseat was a grocery bag full of disposable diapers, a loaf of bread and a box of baby biscuits. So, a quick stop by the store, clip me, then home to momma. That's confidence! I walked around the car, took the ticket in two fingertips and pulled it out. I unlocked the door, slipped inside and starting it up, pulled away.

I drove out to Fleishhacker Zoo and parking along the street, cleaned the wheel and locks, handles and left the wiped keys visible on the floor. I got out and walking for a bit caught the L-Taraval car and rode to Duboce and Church to pick up the N-Judah back home. I was starving so grabbed some spanakopita and a sandwich from the Greek on Irving next to the neighborhood fern bar. I walked over to 6th Avenue and back home.

With Sylvia gone, those steps were just going to get higher, longer and lonelier. I cried when I got upstairs, and started to get some shit together to lay low at Jacks flat. In my head I heard Clovis mocking me…'Sylvia, where for art thou, Sylvia?' Then another voice asked a question.

If Elihu wants you dead, do you think Clovis is that far behind?

Chapter 42

I called François and told him lets meet at the roadhouse, old times sake. I wasn't sure he'd bite the way things were going, me calling, obviously not dead. The breaks had come in my direction to a certain point and I wasn't sure how much he knew.

Matranga had been in to see me with a footlocker a couple of his apes were hauling behind them. He motioned for me to open the safe and I did, walking out of the office to smoke and bullshit with the crew and monthly customers rolling into work. I didn't know if he were loading or unloading and I wasn't giving away a whole lotta fucks on that anyway. The less I knew about his business, the better.

The two goons walked out, one guy carrying the locker so it must've been a delivery. Matranga came out next and taking out his Pall Malls lit one up.

"Been fucking hot hasn't it?" He exhaled.

I just sort of grunted and watched the crew taking care of the incoming cars, driving up and down the ramps.

"This is a good performer, the Pan-American. You guys do alright." He just stood there, and it was creeping me out. Were we bonding?

"You were in 'Nam, right?"

"Yes, I was. I did two tours." Now would he tell me he was too, or that he *wanted* to go.

"I bet you fucked a ton of that good pussy there, huh?" He elbowed me. I gave him an obligatory *mea culpa* smile.

"Yeahhh...I know you did. Hey listen, if you still like them LBFM's then go here. Very discreet, very clean, very quiet. *Very* fine." He laughed here. " So seriously, stop in." He gave me a card, signed with his name.

"Give this to the pineapple at the door or the big one who looks like a island gorilla with dead eyes. He'll hook you up."

The card was from the Castle Street house that Francois had met me at.

"Do you own it?"

"Nooo...but they did us a huge solid and we use it for...things. The big guy runs it and some deep-pocketed blue blood owns the property. They needed permission, and hey, they scratch us and we scratch them back. So, my name on that card means it's for free. Enjoy." He walked away, buttoning his suit coat, and then slicking back the sides of his hair with both hands.

And that was that. Serendipity seemed to have turned her back on Francois.

I sat in the office, doing my day job and out of curiosity I looked over at the safe. The only two people in the world who had the combo were Matranga and I. Not even the bookkeeper. So I pulled my rolly chair on wheels over to it and spun the dial. The combo was Dom's birthday that he had set so he'd never forget it. I didn't think Matranga even knew the meaning. My jaw must've opened wide before I realized the office door wasn't even locked. I got up and did that quickly. The bundles were in denominations of hundred dollar notes and each was two bricks thick. I'd have to bust one to figure out how much a bundle was. Just stacked all neat and tidy. I took a deep breath and shut the door, spinning the tumblers.

Damn!

I finally got a return on my phone call. "Hey, howzit, Remy?" His gruff voice seemed tired.

"Let's meet. Long time, no beer."

Pregnant pause. "Bayshore too damn far, brah. Stay inna city." I knew he was calling from North Beach.

"I always drink at the Buddha Bar on Grant."

"Good call, like maybe, 8, 8:30?'

"Works for me." And he hung up. It took more shape. I kept playing Matranga's words in my head. The missing piece. The reasons. I took a small photo I had of Sylvia. I kept looking at it until I felt sorry for myself.

I'd stopped stashing my bike deep in the Pan-American and kept it down on the main level at the ready. I couldn't rely on MUNI to save my ass if I got into a pinch. I imagined asking people on the streetcar islands on Market if I could take cuts because someone was trying to kill me! I needed to be lightweight, highly portable and able to operate. Even as cumbersome as the .45 was I took to wearing my windbreaker always, concealing my holster.

I went to dinner at the American café and did the usual; veal Parmesan and wine. Afterwards, enjoying an anisette, I thought of my impending meeting with Francois. I had come out of the American and ran full into Marta, Sylvia's roommate.

"How are you?" I asked lamely. I could tell I was probably the last guy she wanted to see.

"I'm okay, but I don't want to talk Remy. I don't know what you did to that girl, but you hurt her bad. She's down in Guyana trying to get her crazy mother home. Quit work, quit school, everything. Bye." And she turned and just walked.

In a blacker mood, I rode slowly into Chinatown, and knowing it would be impossible finding a real parking spot, I parked next to a clementina box halfway up the block where construction was taking place.

He looked the same. No heavier, no lighter, same beater aloha shirt he probably purchased when Hilo Hattie's opened in '63. He slowly smiled as he saw me, and lifted a huge forearm off the bar with his hand ready to shake.

"Hey, howzit, braddah? Long time but was busy, eh. What get?" He looked genuinely happy to see me.

"Not too much, same 'ol same 'ol. You know."

The bar man came over with two long necked, sweating beers.

"Semper fi."

"Semper fi." He took a drink, "Ahh...hey I'm glad to see you, Remy." He said sounding relieved.

I drank, but kept my eye on him, "You look tired, brah. Too much business these days? Whattya have now, three different houses and whatever collateral you do?"

"I'm keeping busy, yea. I'm in da City a lot now. I even bring Lorna up. She at da North Beach house now but I know you involved."

"Not anymore. She left me. *Ce la vie* say the old folks..." I smiled at him. It wasn't a pretty smile.

He laughed, but not heartily, "Well den, maybe you drop by and see about her."

"Wanna know why she left me?" I couldn't keep the edge out of my voice so didn't try.

"No, don' wanna, Remy. That's a nunmy business." He was looking at me, trying to figure it out.

"So, if I want to drop up to see Lorna, I guess it won't cost me anything if I give you this...because it is *your* business, brah." I took out Matranga's card. "This is your business. Small world, eh? We both have the same boss." I laughed, and that wasn't pretty either.

The goose had walked over his grave. He downed the rest of his beer in one swallow. He wiped his mouth, took a breath then spoke, "I tell him not to, but he's been *lolo* doin' blow nonstop and paranoid cuz he tinks you know too much. Also thinks you poking Mona, and he calls you da mudshark. I tell him, no…don't go der, but he no *akamai*. But den Justin's wife call Elihu and crying cuz no phone call from him, nothin' and I know you did him, told him again was a stupid move and he go stone haole and start packing his shit up. Started beefing with Mona and slap her bad, she donno he put a hit on you. Donno if he fly or what. I'm sorry brah, it wasn't me and when I hear Justin all quiet I know he's pau and you're okay." He just sounded tired and earnest but it didn't matter.

"You two the whole way. You whispered to Matranga or some other guys working your book about this little out of the way property of Elihu's that you both saw could be beneficial. Another house of girls, in solid with *these* guys, and your connections in the Bay Area helping them distribute *their* shit because the Marin County competition had been shut down. The Boys are once in awhile down south, but these guys are like 7-11, never closed. No payday for the Boys or anybody who invested. Fucking Elihu," I laughed, "All that fucking money he has and still doesn't want to lose anything on a deal he rigged for failure." I paused and drank, "So how much of a tribute did you get for stopping all of the blow from killing their market?"

He stared ahead; "Da house, free pass to operate, and we all get in bed togetha for various tings…and distribution."

"And that placed Jack in prison, and got his brother killed…even though the Boys sent Justin to Panama, he wasn't taking orders from them, was he?" His dead grey eyes looked thru me, "Thanks for the beer," I said.

He grabbed my forearm to hold me for a second as I rose to stand.

"So where does it stand?"

"Justin is out in Benicia. I guess it's a little crowded out there from what I hear, so he'll have some company. He had my home address, my girlfriend's address and how the fuck did he get that? Someone, maybe Mona or one of your girls stalking us, stalking *her!*" Francois blinked. " Where does it stand? We're *pau*. Don't ever let me see you again. Remember, I've been working for these guys a long time, and if you're not one of them, you're shit. Enjoy your life." I finally stood, straightened out and shifted in my coat, realigning my holster. He watched me and knew I was strapped.

"Remy, I..." I held up my hand. I turned and walked out. I had that part of the puzzle but I didn't have the part about killing Nico. That would mean finding Elihu. The Filbert house would be empty, and after riding by it after Chinatown reinforced that thought. But I parked up the street and walking up to it could not see any lights.

I did break into the mailbox and took everything there.

Chapter 43

Lorna told me the story, breathless and half in shock when she finally arrived. After leaving me, Francois came back earlier than expected to the Castle Street house and immediately went into defensive mode when he saw that his lookout/bouncer was nowhere to be seen. He was slow walking thru the house, and trying to be as quiet as a 290 lb. man could be on old wood floors when he took the first round after hearing the loud pop. The tennis shoe pimp who'd been working Meilani hard to come to his stable had infiltrated the house with another wannabe gangster and after getting the drop on the bouncer, with Meilani's help, had tied him up and placed him in a closet of cleaning gear. All the girls, four in total including Lorna and Meilani were locked into an upstairs bedroom with the idea his new girlfriend would keep the others in line. Ke'Andre, the shooter, had lay in wait for Francois. The plan was for the other shooter, Wendell, to catch Francois in a crossfire, but at the onset of the shooting he ran back upstairs.

The first shot was pure adrenalin, poorly aimed and lodged in one of François' massive thighs, with KeAndre shouting loudly, "Meliani's *my* bitch, fucking pineapple motherfucker!" The second and third went into a love handle and grazed a hip. The next two hit pay dirt in upper chest and neck but he never got off another round as by this time Francois was on him and choking him out.

Hearing the shots from upstairs, the girls were in a panic. Then had already cursed Meilani for her transgressions, and Lorna started slapping her, fearing her benefactor and master was shot dead. Somehow, Ke'Andre got the slip on a staggering Francois, and screaming for Wendell ran his super clean converse All-Stars at high speed upstairs unlocking the bedroom. He peeled the other girls off Meilani, grabbed her and made for the back porch, cursing out Wendell as he ran. Francois took the route thru the kitchen and up the back stairs met the two as they started coming down the back steps.

"Motherfucker!" Was all Ke'andre got out as François grabbed him by the throat in one hand and open handed with the other slapped Meilani unconscious. Ke'Andre's hands were free and with the one trying to pull the massive hand off his throat he pulled a switchblade from a front pocket and stabbed Francois in the top of his shoulder sinking it behind his clavicle. Grunting, Francois used his other free hand, grabbed the dangling man by the crotch and lifting him threw him down onto the cement lanai from upstairs. He landed awkwardly, his femur snapping in two on his right leg, the bone sticking bloodily out of the rip in his slacks. François then pulled the knife out of his shoulder and cursed. He bent, slowly, and grabbing Meilani by the hair dragged her back into the house. When the other three women saw him they gasped. He was bleeding from multiple places and scared the shit out of them. He asked where Kaipo, the doorman was, and Sharona went and unlocked the cleaning closet, helping him untie his bonds. Lorna and Poelani started to clean up Francois, who had lit a cigarette and had sat down on the toilet. He'd thrown Meilani in the old iron bathtub, still unconscious.

"Jesus, Francois, how many times he shoot you?" Lorna said breathlessly.

"Dumbass...shot me widda twenty-two. Shit!" He turned to the other

Polynesian girl, "Poei, go outside, downstairs, see how that boy doin' or if he's *make*." Scared and eyes wide, she obeyed.

"You gonna need a doctor, this wound in your shoulder is deep cut and gonna be infected," Lorna told him.

"What'd he tink he gonna do? Take my house and girls?" He looked at Lorna, his eyes grey and dead, small and blinking in the big head reminded her of pig's eyes. "You know about dis, Lorna?"

"No! Meilani seeing this boy on the side. Meet him on the street grocery shopping and he promise her the better life and all that shit. Damn Francois, we don't know. She confess it all when he lock us up, trying to make us understand, so we cannot warn you." She trembled looking at the bullet hole in his side as blood slowly oozed out, "You need a doctor, seriously."

He nodded. Poelani came back in. " He's not *make* but he's laying there annit's horrible. The bone in his leg sticking out of his pants, big puddle of blood. I don't wanna be that close to him" About now Meilani started coming to.

"Where's dat othah boy who he yelled for and help tie up Kaipo?" Poelani asked, just as Kaipo came to the door, eyes wide seeing Francois condition.

"Damn, boss…you okay? Want I should call one doctor or take you to ER?"

Lorna had found him cowering in one of the closets across the hall. He had fled there when he witnessed Ke'Andre's attempts to kill Francois and saw it wasn't going well. He was under a blanket in the closet. When Lorna had lifted the blanket he handed her his gun. Francois got help getting off the toilet and they all went to see Wendell. Francois held his hand out without speaking and just as quietly, Kaipo handed him a knife and he took the girls back into the other room. Lorna said Francois was alone with this guy for five minutes then returned to the bathroom.

"Kaipo, get dat *bambucha* blue tarp, go downstairs and if you need, finish him and then cover it good. Hang 'we out' sign den come back, and get showah curtains from all *benjos* and call Raymond come help you get da guy outta da closet. We take a ride later tomorrow when dark." He scratched his head, flexed the stabbed shoulder and winced. "Poei, call dis numbah," And he told her, making her memorize, "And tell him I need help now, get off da okole and make it happen. You girls go downstairs and cook someting, eh?" He went back to the bathroom Meilani was in.

They never saw Meilani again.

I had given Lorna my number back in the day if there were ever an emergency, or a bust, and either Francois was pinched or out of pocket. Later that night she called me. Her voice was stressed and the fear was thick as a brick. The girls had stayed in the house, cleaning up the debris from the fight while Kaipo and Raymond went about getting the bodies ready for disposal. I wondered if they'd take the same trip to Benicia the Weasel and I did.

"Remy it was so scary. I'm frightened stay in that house. I wanna go back to Daly City, but cannot go. Francois calls this guy from Pacific Heights and told him about his wounds. Then by Jesus, he just drive himself somewhere after being shot and stabbed!" That whole report sounded sort of novel in the context of Francois. "Can I stay with you tonight? I got money for a cab. You live out by the park I remember you saying?"

She sounded pathetic and scared to death so I said yea, and gave her my address, telling her I'd leave the door unlocked just come in. I went into my living room, poured a drink, and went to the Sherlock and tapped out a couple of lines. It reminded me of my use the night Justin came in and the repulsive look I got from Sylvia. I took another couple of hits. The

Jameson's in my glass took the edge off the coke. I put on some 'Trane, hoping to find some normalcy and also formulate a few questions about the business there. She'd been with him over seven years and had to know where a few of the skeletons were.

Chapter 44

I was in that jazz zone when she finally arrived; my head back, mouth open and two inches of ash on my cigarette. I came out of it as she took the cigarette from between my fingers to tap it off. I rubbed my face, sitting up and tried to give her a smile.

Lora looked like she'd run all the way from North Beach. Her car coat was buttoned up to her chin and her two skinny legs out of the bottom terminated into cheap, pink stained sneakers. Her hair, usually soft and straight looked wild and drunk.

"You need a drink?" I asked.

"Damn, yes. I also need a shower cuz I'm covered in blood." And she opened the car coat looking like a field surgeon in a forward area. She had a paper shopping bag she'd brought that held some clothes that she grabbed from the North Beach house. I pointed to the bathroom and silently she went in, and after a bit I heard the water running.

Francois must've been a mess. I picked up her discarded clothes and placed them in a dry cleaning bag I had left over and took them outside and around the corner to the shitcans used by the fern bar. Before I went back I looked up into the night sky of San Francisco. There was one long lone stratus cloud that looked like a crocodile with numerous heads just hovering up there. The moon was three quarters full and as always just passive and unassuming, minding its own. I missed Sylvia badly. It'd been a few days since I took a box of her things and left them on her stoop, ringing the bell and leaving. I'd hoped she'd call but no such luck. It was cowardly, yes, but a gesture I had to make. Now with Marta's revelation, it made me feel even more foolish. I went back upstairs.

Lorna had on a towel, combing her hair out with my brush. I figured to just throw her an old tee for a nightshirt she being so petite it would look like a dress.

"Remy, you have a girl now, yea?"

"No, I did, but not anymore. You hungry?" I changed the subject.

"That soap isn't a man's soap and there's a thong panty on the back of the door under a towel. Why no more?"

I just looked at her, "It didn't work out. I can scramble some eggs for you."

"*Mahalos*, I'm starving. Today and tonight were just damn long and ugly."

I'd never really had a normal conversation with Lorna. It wasn't that type of thing. I'd fall by the place in Daly City, and we'd maybe share some *saimin*, take a shower and fuck. Then I'd fly, living the 'not here for a long time, just here for a good time' credo, but I would leave her small gifts or new lingerie. And now here we were discussing a multiple homicide and mutilation like an old married couple watching the news.

I scrambled her eggs and made some toast. I kept snorting and drinking. When she was done, we smoked and she finally seemed to relax. I was buzzing inside, on fire. We looked at each other.

"Long time since I see you," she said. I nodded. "Francois told me you had a woman, wouldn't see you around anymore. He said she wasn't white and I felt good about that."

"Yea, that's true. Lets leave it there. Tell me about tonight." And she did, working her way thru it. When she got to the point of Kaipo and

Raymond bringing Ke'Andre's body inside so birds and feral cats wouldn't disturb it, I asked:

"What was Meilani thinking?"

"Shoots, who knows from that girl! That guy, her boyfriend the street pimp was crazy. Locking us away, I was so scared I thought I'd end up like those nurses in Chicago, the only one left that Filipina girl who hid under the bed!" I could see the fear creep back into her.

"Ever feel like Francois would kill you?"

"After tonight, shit yes. Remy, he ain't human. After seeing him shot and stabbed and just acting like, eh…no biggy." She looked around. "You have a nice place. Looks…manly."

I thanked her. "He ever meet a guy at the North Beach house…" And here I described Elihu. She nodded yes, he's the guy Poelani called. I pressed it. "So what'd they do? Ever hear anything they said?"

She bit her lip, a little kid in class searching for the answer to a question. "They once talk about how happy the Italians were. I didn't get it since I didn't see any Italian johns, just Italian guys who come and discuss business. The only Italian who come and fucks is this guy named Phil, and no way in hell does he want to be called a john. He's a part owner."

"What kinds of guys come there?"

"All sorts, but these guys dress different, all in suits. And we pretend we're all Asian, but most mixed or part…you know, poi dogs. In Daly City guys always looked like they get off work with nametags or sneak away from the wife—these guys always dressed well, well groomed, even the underwear look expensive. One guy who goes with me tells me I should work in Miami. Better weather, nice and warm like the islands and better clientele."

"So not Italian?"

"No, these guys were Spanish or from Spanish places. I can tell from living here in Cali."

"What else did these guys do, talk about?" I figured around the women they'd feel uninhibited, and like big boys always needing to impress.

"They would joke, my john and François, about it snowing in Miami and this guy had told me how warm it is. Don't make sense!"

It was starting to. "That guy I described, so how many times did he fall by the house that you can remember?"

"Hmmm…he was a weirdo. Smoked these fat cigarettes too. Dunno, maybe four, five times."

"Did he ever…?"

"Oh yea, he goes with Poelani all the time. She's Tahitian and he make her speak French." I had a flash of Gomez Addams and Morticia. I wondered if Mona spoke French.

"How about this guy?" I took out Justin's driver's license.

"Dat guy! He came last week. I'll never forget him, cuz his wife and baby came too. Francois calls him trailer trash and cracker after they go. He come for a payoff, Francois give him an envelope." She started to yawn. "Remy, where can I sleep?"

'Go in my room. I'm out here on the couch. There's a spare toothbrush in the medicine cabinet, and I'll give you a tee to sleep in"

I was going thru my drawer and found a large tee for her and as I turned around the towel was gone. She was lying, one leg up, exposed.

"You know Remy, you're the only guy I ever kiss on the lips since I come here. Ever."

I shook my head, "That's sweet, Lorna. I'm honored, now here, this'll be like a nightshirt."

"Its your bed. I miss you coming to Daly City." Then I wondered if it was all bullshit and François would come thru the door later like Justin and do me. My coke paranoia was on the large side that night. "You think I'm pretty?"

"Yes, Lorna, I've always felt you were."

"Well, you know, even if lady has wacky face like a prawn, you can eat the body and throw the head away." She teased.

"Go to bed." I walked out and shut the door. I settled into the front room and taking out my Sherlock and pouring three fingers started thinking of finding Elihu Fuqua and asking him why he had my cousin killed. After brainstorming to no end, I just passed out. The bourbon had beaten the coke. Sometime in the middle of the night, Lorna had come in, pulled me by the arms to stand me up and with an arm around me pulled me to my bed, taking my pistol out of my fingers and holding it. I didn't fight her when she insisted. I just lay down and held her and slept. She experienced a nightmare later about when the two black men were broken into pieces and taken away.

I could relate.

Doc Krinberg

Chapter 45

My problem was work. I had obligations to people that scared me more than a wounded Francois, or an Elihu in hiding. I could be secure only up to a point, as anyone could walk into the garage and ask for the manager, then put me down and That's all, folks. But to start skipping work and leaving the safe unattended during what those guys feel is a crucial time was something totally different. And way scarier.

I just had to carry on as if nothing happened. Francois' bad luck wasn't on me, and Elihu's move that had failed actually gave me a little respite. He couldn't run to the D-boys for protection. I could envision it.

"Uhh, so why did you order a hit on Remy? Oh, right, he found out you scotched *our* last run, lost us like half a million and were involved in clipping the mule's brother because he *talked* to a DEA guy and you got scared? Hmm…yea sure, we'll help you." I played that in my head and had to laugh. But still, I was concerned about a wounded Francois and what that would mean for his network and if my name was on a list somewhere as a KA. But I hoped he was the type of guy who kept his rolodex in his head.

I looked at Lorna in bed and wondered what she'd look like in twenty years. I wondered if I had twenty years in me, and if it really mattered now after the Justin incident. Lorna on Sylvia's side of the bed made my stomach hurt. Then the phone rang.

"It's me." The Weasel.

"Hey, are you still incognito or have you talked to the Board members?"

"A c-couple. I'm inching my way back. I tried to c-call you at Noe, but no dice."

"I decided to come home. I can't go into hiding, and I think the threat is pau . I'm still game to talk to Fuqua and watch him drop water."

"That might b-be fun to watch."

"Listen all kidding aside I have an update for you. Last night some street hustler who's been working on one of Francois' girls in North Beach popped a few caps into him. All reports are that before mentioned pimp and associate's parts will be probably drifting in the vicinity of Angel Island soon. Francois got in touch with Elihu after he was fucked up and drove himself to an undisclosed location. No way would he go to the ER. They must have some doc they know on the QT."

He whistled, "Dayummm...that's c-crazy. How d-did you get all this?"

"One of his Daly City girls is a friend and working North Beach, was in there for the entire horror show and dig this—she described a guy who's been banging one of the girls there regularly; Elihu. Lots of loose talks with cartel like characters and also ID'd Justin who came for a payoff. Came to the house with his wife and kid."

"F-f-uck!" I would've stuttered too hearing all that. "So what're you d-doing?"

"Work. I hate to sound like romantic confessions but I basically have no life but work, and not pissing off my bosses as I hobnob with desperados. But I want to find Elihu, and see where that goes. I took a pile of his mail and there might be a clue in there."

"And Francois?"

"This is my thinking; he had nothing to do with Nick. Yes, for sure with the plan to get Jack dropped, and if the guys in Marin know that, about the two of them, then seriously I guess they're going to be putting feelers out too. So tell me about this 'inching?' "

"I've been d-direct with C-corky. I've known him the longest. He grew up in the San Joaquin like me and while he d-doesn't look it, he's also Armenian too. I explained my actions and a few things in P-p-panama, and after your info, dropped a few words on the North B-beach house and a few things I found out on my own. I had a talk with Justin's wife." I wondered if he recorded it and played it back for Corky, or if she were even still alive.

At this point, I didn't care one way or another.

Chapter 46

I had started to wonder what Mona did during her day. I had no clue if she worked, ran a business, or just stayed home and painted her toenails. When Elihu had first met her at Enrico's, she was dancing up the street at The Condor Club in the late 60's. Before that, no one knew anything about her with the exception of her letting me know we both had Viet Nam in our pasts. Now that I was a mail thief, I had to do something with my ill-gotten letters. The bulk was business items for Elihu, but they listed property addresses for work rendered in two houses; one on Telegraph Hill and the other on Russian Hill. I wondered if Elihu had ever used Chappy for the woodwork in the Pacific Heights house, and if perhaps that's how he met his demise. Did Chappy get too chappy with Mona? I took down those addresses and then pondered over the one not addressed to him. It was from a retired Colonel Monte Bohannon, Sr., from Sagamihara, Japan. It was addressed to Mrs. Mona Bohannon. I just stared at it. But I couldn't open it. I'd check out the two houses in the city, because I truly believed they'd go batshit hiding in Stinson or the Russian River property. Both were city creatures.

I'd let Lorna stay at my flat and promised to take her back later. She'd called the North Beach house; got one of the island guys who was pissed off she'd fled. She talked him off the edge explaining how frightened she was and he bought it. He told her the boss was recuperating and wanted business as usual to continue regardless of what happened. Three murders were just a speed bump around these parts. She said she needed another day, and he acquiesced.

In the midst of all of this I had to carry on as normal. I had cleaned and reloaded my .45 and sported a very low profile shoulder rig for it and kept a spare clip in my jacket pocket. I was living with it now. I thought if it were possible, maybe the Weasel could find a silencer for it. While he had become a kindred spirit, I knew his obligations and roots were with the Disney Boys and things could go south in a hurry. I wondered if he felt the same with me. I was sure he did.

Lorna and I ate Chinese from the place around the corner because I wished to stick close to home. I'd give her a ride to North Beach the next day, the sooner the better. While we ate she just chatted. She'd started in the sex trade her freshman year in high school in Aiea and knew one thing; she didn't need to live in Hawaii and change sheets in Waikiki or keep being molested by her uncle. She and a girlfriend cut classes one day to go hang at Blaisdell Park and met Francois there who happened to be on O'ahu for business. He was at the park meeting up with some old friends, playing ukuleles and just hanging out. The girls hung out with them because they had reefer and beer. He took her off to the side and talked story to her. She decided to work for him and the next day after gathering a few things at home flew back with him. She also liked that she didn't have to fuck him. He never asked, never demanded or inferred it. I tried to see Francois, as benevolent enabler but couldn't. He was a pimp who wore a different hat and while he treated the girls with a warped sense of *aloha* he was still a pimp. I knew underneath it, and especially after Lorna's tale of woe, he was capable of anything.

Her story, for some reason put me in a black mood. I started drinking early. Lorna didn't like bourbon so I had bought her some wine. She asked why I didn't have a TV and I laughed that I was stupid enough. I started to get morose. Sylvia's words came back to me from that day. The description of the fly caught by that thing in the silk, that winter spider who saved its hunger until it exploded; like I exploded on Justin. I felt it was unfair as Justin had it coming, and the fly didn't. Or did it? I thought of those responsible for Nick and I knew for sure *they* deserved it. The morose turned to anger; a slow red burn like a fire on a mountain seen from miles away. I took out my Sherlock. Lorna saw me and moved closer. I cut some lines out for her on the cheap flat mirror I used. She took the rolled bill I offered and we did that until we needed to stop and drink a bit. Lighting a cigarette I felt the need for something with an edge and 'Let it Bleed' was still on the turntable. My killing album, I couldn't deal with that memory, maybe something familiar, not as raw. I threw on 'The Rolling Stones: Now!' I went over to her and took the cigarette out of her mouth and pulled her sleeper tee over her head, her thick hair falling back to her shoulders. Sitting topless I poured some more onto the mirror and started chopping it. She stood up, cigarette between her teeth and started dancing to the music. I kept snorting, sitting there with no shirt, a shoulder holster and jeans. Lorna pulled her panties up from both sides as she danced and they split her lips in two. She did moves to 'Little Red Rooster' moving with the slide guitar and turning her back to me and giving me a slow lap dance. I visited Lorna a long time in Daly City and this was all new. We were out of school here and I cranked the music again. She unbuttoned my jeans and pulled them off and we both met over the mirror to snort the remaining lines there. I pulled my index finger over the glass and put it in her mouth and I thought of the spider. Then Jennifer. Then 'Mona' came on and she was back in my head. I pulled Lorna to me and she danced in my face, her arousal strong, as I tapped out more coke. I was having trouble cutting it and so I just used the razor to negotiate some huge fat lines. I pushed her head down to the mirror and she did two up throwing her head back, one finger under her nose. Inside me something started snapping, and I grabbed her by the hips and turned her. I pulled her panties so hard they ripped and she wiggled out of them with super hopped up giggles at sonic speed, she bent over touching her toes her hair hanging like a flag in a windless sky she crooked a 'come hither' finger at me upside down from between her legs. I took one of my fingers and collecting as much coke on it I could I slid it down in between her asscheeks, inside of her... *'I tell you Mona what I'm gonna do..'*

Yes. I was the spider.

Chapter 47

Matranga visited me and had a very large mailbag some linebacker carried into the office.

"Wow," I said, " I think the safe is finally full."

"Yea, looks like it. But it's temporary, maybe two weeks at the most." He looked at me, "You okay, Karras? You look like you lost weight."

"I'm okay." Thinking a guy like Matranga could give two fucks about my health. "Say, I went to that house you recommended. Damn good. Is that big Moke guy a friend of yours?"

Matranga made a face, "That pineapple nigger? Fuck him. He's temporary and doesn't know it. Too old school for me. When and which girl did you go with? Remember?" Now he was into the conversation.

"Right after you gave me the card. I think her name was Lurleene or something? Finer than frog hair as we used to say in-country." I gave him my best Gomer Pyle smile.

He smiled back, "I like how fucking smooth their skin is. Fuck, some of these Irish twists here in the city use Ivory soap and feel like #4 sandpaper. Those girls are like honey."

"I did talk to a guy there who was seeing a Tahitian girl. He had a funny name, and anyway he was talking about how he was the true owner of the property and how he put the kibosh on a group of guys in Marin country to get there, meaning the house." I shook my head. "Some guys."

Matranga looked like I just farted in a closed car, "Did he?" I just shrugged.

"But hey, thanks for the card, most appreciated."

He was still turning over my words about Elihu, "Yea, yea. No problem. You do us good, Remy." He turned back to the safe, "Anyway, in like two weeks a panel truck will show up after the morning rush. You'll put a couple of guys on break and then we'll see about transporting all of that out of there. Until then, just keep the porch light on, all right?"

"All right."

And he and the linebacker went out and the crew fought to grab his Chrysler, as Matranga was always good for a five-dollar tip.

Lorna took the streetcar downtown and I told her I'd pick her up atop the Stockton Street tunnel after work and then drop her at the North Beach house. She was there when I cruised down Pine. I don't know how she felt when she woke up but we didn't talk before we finally fell asleep. Some things are better left alone, I figured. When she got on the back of the bike I felt her warm dry lips on my neck and then pulled herself up into me. I had a momentary flash to the night before and then just gunned the bike.

I dropped her at the bottom of Castle and said goodbye. I headed to the first address on Russian Hill. It was on an amazingly steep part of Chestnut. And the property looked vacant. There wasn't a realtor sign up but there was a permit from the city of construction in the front window. There were no telltale piles of shit on the front steps to speak to a tenant. I pulled into the driveway and in the back. Peeking over the fence I saw a couple of sawhorses and cut drywall. There were irregular carpet remnants, cut two by fours and scattered paint cans. Definite remodeling.

The Telegraph Hill address was on Child Street. I flew by it on the bike and then uphill carefully turned around to find a safe place to park where it wouldn't fall over. I found a good stand two doors down that didn't have a car on it. I dismounted, opened my coat a little and stretched looking down at the view on this part of the City. As I turned back he hit me hard enough I came off my feet, scattering my keys one way and leaving me sprawled on the ground, jacket partially opened and the butt of my gun protruding. Francois, in a flannel shirt and sweater, a huge bandage on his neck picked up my keys and sitting astride my bike it looked like a kid's Big Wheel underneath him.

"Eh, no blame me, brah. Its on Elihu..." And kicking it over he pushed off the stand and hitting second then third gear down the hill, he may as well have been going warp speed.

I had no time to do anything but sit up and watch. He wanted to make a left turn but couldn't negotiate it; too fast, no skill. Running the stop he was hit head-on and then airborne. The sound of the bike hitting metal hurt but then he flew into the adjacent Stop sign head first neck up he decapitated himself instantly. That sound I will never forget, like a watermelon dropped out of a three-story window. The driver got out of the car and started freaking out, and by then quite a few people issued out onto the intersection. One older guy appeared out of nowhere and helped me up.

The rest of the evening was a mess. I had to stand fast for the police when they showed. I had no time to ditch my .45 and standing there with an empty holster would be just as incriminating if not downright embarrassing, so I zipped up my jacket to half-mast thanking the cool night air and my interviews were conducted just like that...'Yea, I was going for a ride to Coit Tower, heard a noise in my engine, turned around and found a safe place to park to check it out...' A nosey neighbor, the old duffer who helped me corroborated that...' Then as I got off my bike I'm cold cocked and then this giant gets on my bike, goes too fast hits a car and then the stop sign. That's it.' That taken into account, I was Remy

Karras, with an outstanding driving record, no warrants, stand up ex-marine, now a garage manager with a union card and solid citizen and can we help you in any way Mr. Karras? Do you need to see a doctor? Even though it hurt like a hundred toothaches from where he hit me, I declined and also declined the news people who started swarming around as well.

I took a cab home after my poor bike was towed to the vehicle impound for evidence. I was given a card and a slip for when I could retrieve it for repairs. The ambulance people gave back to the woman who loaned her towel out of decency to cover Francois' head and she promptly dumped it in her trash. As they loaded him up before I left, both parts, I just put my hand up in the goodbye attitude and whispered a last semper fi.

Later, I called Elihu's house even if he wasn't there and left a message.

"Francois passed away." Well, he did, sort of.

And then I made another call.

"So how are you, cousin?" I asked cheerfully.

"I'm well," he hesitated and I could hear Meredith's muffled tone in the background. "To what do I owe this pleasure? How's Jack?"

"He's fine. His finances are good so far and his mail to his folks is running smooth. Has he written you, or written you off?"

"What's that supposed to mean? Have something to say to me Remy?" He was annoyed but I could also hear the apprehension rising in his voice.

"Listen. Francois's dead and your alter ego is in hiding from me, and I'm sure you know why. And by now probably all the Boys are looking for him too. Tell me how deep in it were you, oh cousin of mine? By the way, I said hi to Chappy. Remember him? Okay, you can ask Meredith what to say now."

Clovis hung up. I turned to the Weasel.

"That went well, don't you think?"

"He's a b-bit coldhearted for a relative, d-don't you think? Did he always have a hard-on for you and the two b-b-brothers?"

"Seems so. I'm at a crossroads here now. A personal Rubicon."

Arthur Berberian asked me again what I thought.

"I'm pretty sure the Boys will scoop up Elihu and deal with him. He cost them a lot of money and prestige, not to mention problems. Karma took care of Francois for all of us. Are you sure they're okay with Justin?"

"Yea. They really c-c-could care less. A man and his c-castle, and all that rot. They c-can find guys for wet work, believe me."

"I suppose. We couldn't attract enough assholes to the Marines and they kept showing up on the doorstep."

"The elephant in the room is C-Clovis. What do you plan to do about him?"

"Where do you get an elephant extermination license?"

He took a pad of paper and a pen and started writing what I thought was a number or a name. He handed it to me. It was a quick doodle of an elephant with an X over it.

"This w-work for you?"

Doc Krinberg

Chapter 48

I'd hit a dead end trying to run down Mona sadly, because I felt she could be exploited in locating Elihu. Then I wondered if I shouldn't change my opinion of her. The thought of Mona being slapped around by Elihu made me angry. She didn't seem like the type to take it and like it. The only thing positive was the Telegraph Hill house they let Francois shelter in that I spoiled. Lorna called me after they got the news about his death and it appeared that both Matranga and some big bald guy (Polli) grabbed some initiative and took over the house, and after talking to the other girls and security guys, Kaipo and Raymond, he installed them as temp bosses in the Peninsula houses. Lorna went back into circulation in Daly City where she was comfortable and asked me to drop in. That door shut the other night.

Matranga. He could help me find Elihu, the owner of the property.

And Elihu? What the hell did he think he was doing? Rich, entitled and a poster boy for cocaine psychosis and grandiosity, was the short lived run at the North Beach house an ego fantasy fulfilled? An 'I'll show you' moment?' Hanging with mob and SA cartel guys from Miami was some sort of validation? I couldn't figure it out, but he certainly knew how to be careless with other people's lives and belongings.

How could I squeeze Elihu out of Matranga without telling him why? Better yet, how could I clip Clovis?

I had a free weekend coming since I'd become a single drunk man again. My bike had been released and was under the smokewrench at the Triumph-Norton-BSA shop on Van Ness. I needed wheels.

"Is all you have that Ford station wagon?"

"That's b-been gone since the day after B-Benicia. It's scrap. I'm driving a beater now; inconspicuous in this area, don't you think?"

He was right and how could I argue with a master chameleon. I needed something reliable with no receipts, or paper and I knew only one place to go.

"Want to buy it or borrow it?" He asked.

"I need it for a weekend, no more. No less."

"Why should I?"

"Because I'm going to remove a tick from our collective hides, okay?" I finished my beer. "Any luck finding *your* friend from Pacific Heights?"

He grimaced, "No. And that's a bit of an embarrassment. I'm still confused as to what all that was about. His damn family has more money than fucking Croesus."

"Go figure." I went for it. "This North Beach house that he and Francois placed all their bets on—there's a guy who may know. He's connected, a made guy. His name is Phil Matranga." I dropped the card he gave me in the garage.

He picked it up. "Seriously, Remy, I'm sorry for both Jack and his brother. This all didn't have to happen."

"Thanks. True that."

He held out the keys to his '67 Mustang. "Fill it before you turn it back in."

The Winter Spider

"Thanks, Corky."

I didn't ask the Weasel where he got the drop piece with the silencer for me and he didn't offer. The fact that he got it so quickly and chauffeured me to Corky's for a vehicle told me he was back in the saddle again. The only thing I felt bad about was not being a fly on the wall when local outlaw and local mob guy discuss Elihu's fate and how much it would cost to give him up. I pictured Matranga explaining to Elihu they'd protect him but he needed to give up the deed and some cash. They'd turn around and get cash from Corky as a finder's fee and then give up Elihu to Corky, and maybe Mona too. Or turn her out. I didn't feel good thinking that might happen.

Along with the car, Corky cut loose with two black beauties. "These babies will keep you up for a twenty-four hour stretch, and forty-eight back to back. You may need a pick me up after your long ass drive to LA." He smiled. I hadn't told him where I was going but he knew exactly what I was doing.

The drive I took started at six p.m. that Friday. It took some time to get thru the traffic and to break out. I opted to 101 and though the drive was longer I wouldn't have to suffer the cows and crop stinks in Stanislaus and Kern counties. Anyway, it would take me closer to where my cousin lived, and after dropping the top south of San Jose, it made it a beautiful drive. I was mildly surprised at the cassettes he owned; Velvet Underground, Dr. John the Night Tripper, Otis Redding, The Doors, some jazz and Beethoven's Piano Concertos.

There was about zero traffic midway and only the occasional trucker. The air was sweet and with the windows up the wind was kept at a minimum. I ate the first black beauty down near Paso Robles. I stopped and got gas. I looked to the west, to the Polonio Pass and gave a small semper fi to James Dean. Down near Oxnard I could feel myself coming onto the amphetamine because I noticed I was speeding and had 'Gris Gris Man' cranked up high. I hit the break with PCH and headed inland towards the Valley, straight thru to Hollywood and my destination. By my reckoning it would be about 3 a.m. when I arrived at Case de Clovis.

Chapter 49

Arthur the Weasel had hooked me up with a Walther P-5 equipped with a 4-inch silencer. I knew they were badass and popular with German cops. I wondered how popular it would be with my duplicitous fucking cousin.

Past Thousand Oaks I started to hit the drunks cruising for coffee shop traffic here on the western rim of the Valley. The black beauty had me feeling that speed heat and it was radiating like I was a nucleus. Making it thru the Valley I drove up to the off ramp. I winded up a few streets hoping they were asleep. I liked the idea of a surprise. At times during the drive I pictured Sylvia's face catching me in that dog act of killing Justin and it relit some dangerous fires inside me. The fire I'd lay at Clovis' feet.

It was dead quiet on their street so I pulled into a curbside spot away from a streetlamp. It was an old neighborhood and the houses had long side driveways going to detached garages that butted up to alleys where people stored their shitcans. The houses were small with Spanish tile roofs and stucco exteriors; typical Southern California gothic. The house I grew up in was like this. The night was beautifully peaceful and the jasmine was blooming, exploding almost overpowering like an older woman who having dulled senses just poured on too much. Walking quietly up the driveway the speed was just making me feel amazing, everything was amplified. I looked up at the kitchen windows, a full head over me and I could see the small night light over the sink burning for the late glass of water or snack. I knew their bedroom was in the back with French doors out to the yard. I went to the back porch where the bulb was burnt and needed replacing. I tried the knob.

Bingo.

Inside I could hear the hum of the refrigerator. I had 'The End' in my head and this was the place for it. I stood still and heard nothing else. I left my shoes pointed at the back door in the kitchen and crept towards the bedroom. There was a bathroom in between two closed doors with a tiny nightlight inside. I knew theirs was on the right pointing to the back of the house. I took a face from the ancient gallery…and opened the door.

Like any old door it creaked a little but the two figures in bed didn't move. There was another small night light in a wall socket on the floor near the closet. I could see Meredith's hair fanned out on the pillow. The gag and cuffs were hers.

I never imagined it to be a fun time. It wasn't.

I pulled into Corky's old barn garage at dusk, Saturday. I took my time driving up the coast, enjoying the pull offs south of Big Sur. The compliments on the Mustang were plentiful. The morning was brilliant and it was just one of those sky's the limits days. Corky came out of his A-frame and with his hands inside his denim coveralls looked like a gentleman farmer. I'd called him an hour out so he could be alone, no surprises with kids and wife or friends. He opened the door for me.

"How'd she run?"

"Beautiful. Just a fine damn machine."

"Any problems?" He raised an eyebrow.

I smiled. "Nope. Brought you a souvenir from LA. I looked at it and it said Corky all over it." He gave me stink eye. I walked to the trunk of the Mustang and he followed. I popped it open and he peeked in. He turned to me and said, "You gotta be shitting me." He turned back to the trunk. "Welcome back, Elihu."

Chapter 50

Polli came by the garage and did a cursory 'hello.' Since Dom had skimmed these guys they were all a little more hands on and I noticed they were all younger too. Matranga and Polli had to be only a few years older than me. Changing of the guard I supposed. Polli asked me how much I thought was in the safe. Where Matranga was a bit more Dale Carnegie, I noticed Polli had some rough edges.

"Dunno, hard to tell. I never look in it. That's Mr. Matranga's business," I watched his eyes. They narrowed a little.

"It's my business too, pal. There's quite a bit in there. A few mill' for sure. You know we're coming up on that pick up."

A few mill', I thought. "Will you or Mr. Matranga be here for that?"

"He'll be here and so will I." He was always pissed off about something. I knew guys in the corps like this. I knew one who is still MIA because he pissed off the wrong person.

"I'll get back to you again." I just nodded like my head was full of dried beans.

I had a few days. Arthur had to come thru on this one big time.

Doc Krinberg

Chapter 51

I enjoyed seeing Meredith wet herself, and in her humiliation she knew it. I felt Jack's joy in how he used to piss her off. Mortified and outraged in her cuffs she could only make noises around her ball gag. I'd improvised with a few of her bras to secure her to the brass rails of the headboard. A dry pair of panties was in Clovis' mouth. They fit easy with more bras and tee shirts for his hands and feet.

Elihu I had to knock out cold.

I sat in front of Clovis and told him I knew he was in on it, that he was culpable and this game they set in motion had killed Nick, crippled his parents...his own aunt and uncle and had pissed off too many people who expected a huge windfall from Jack's return. His total discount of family and associates was just unacceptable.

"You greedy, one-way fuckers have destroyed a lot." I pointed to the floor, where Elihu lay unconscious. "*This* turd has more money than Onassis and yet he thought he was Jean Paul Belmondo or something. He's shit. You're shit." I jerked my head towards Meredith. I looked into Clovis' eyes. "And in your whimsy to clip me, I lost the only fucking thing that mattered to me, so this is what you created, this moment," and I placed my left hand, fingers spread on my chest to indicate he'd purchased ME. "Oh Meredith, where for art thou Meredith?" I smiled, "Sound familiar""

I'd been tying up Clovis after a good bonk on his melon when lo and behold, carrying a baseball bat, Elihu had crept in from the bedroom on the other side of the bathroom. I had turned and picked up the gun and leveled it at him, "A ninja you are not. Strike three, Elihu. Put it down." He did and I used it to give him a sweet concussion.

Turning back to my cousin, "Okay, its confessional time. When I take the panties out of your mouth, if you speak above a whisper, then say tally-ho to Meredith. Understood?" He nodded his head.

How convenient, according to Clovis, that the unconscious guy on the floor cooked it all up. He and Francois had given the first mule a hotshot thru the girl he was banging. Then when it still was in motion it was pure vitriol when Clovis whispered in Jack's ear to jump in. He hated Jack because of how he treated Meredith, and she welcomed it, so why not? Then they all panicked when that DEA guy braced Nick in Panama. The paranoia had kicked in and even though the Boys had sent Justin to Panama, he was bought, head to toe by Elihu and Clovis. They were scared of how I was pushing everyone for Jack's interests and then that dumbass moke Francois had showed me the North Beach house that was supposed to be a secret but that fucker with the semper fi bullshit had opened a can of worms. So, I knew too much. And anyway, according to Elihu and Clovis I was just a fucking mudshark, and Elihu was sure I was also putting the stick to Mona while sleeping with Sylvia and he didn't want to touch her after that. Enter Poelani.

Meredith just couldn't stop the water works, and listening to her noises I flashed on the scorched pillowcase on Justin's head. I told Clovis to keep his mouth shut while I finally got around to tying up Elihu. I had an inspiration, no doubt from the speed, and pulling Meredith's wet panties off I shoved them in Elihu's mouth. Clovis started to hyperventilate.

"Remy...I'm your cousin...we're blood. You can't be thinking what I think you're thinking?" He started pleading. "C'mon, my parents...

Meredith's family."

"You mean thinking what you tried to do...to me? I suppose if I'd held up the time-out sign for Justin, he would've smoked a cigarette and given me a second chance? And I don't like your parents so calm your shit, Clovis." I whispered huskily. He looked at Meredith. "Did you tell Justin to kill Nick? Answer me, be clean and concise."

He was clean and concise.

I had to devise a new logistical plan, as I hadn't counted on Elihu hiding out there. Mona was nowhere on the premises and I'd talk to him about that later as my cousin had no clue either. After they had a falling out she went a different direction and Elihu allowed her to leave. Now I'd have to pull the car up the driveway and carry him out to the trunk which I didn't like as it ran the risk of someone out walking a dog, being naturally nosey at 4 a.m. and writing down a plate or a partial plate or car description. I wasn't happy. I certainly didn't want to leave the car in the alley where a prowl car would definitely stop and ask the universal 'can we help you, sir?'

I went around the house quietly and turned things over, covered a glass framed pic with a coach pillow and broke it, shaking the glass out over the carpet. I went thru Meredith's things, asking her where they were and going by her head and eye directions I took jewelry and a few loose gems, dropping one or two here and there. Pulled out drawers and left them open. I then asked Clovis where the money stash was, and after having to push the silencer muzzle against his forehead hard, I went to the outer hall closet and under the floorboards was pleasantly shocked. A lifetime of scams and deals, take offs and heists were cleanly bundled in almost the same way as the swag in the safe at work. I told him quietly over my shoulder 'the IRS would be pissed off if they found this.' There was also a half a brick of pot, a few pill bottles and what looked like half an ounce of blow. The prize was an old Parabellum Luger from WW2 inside a plastic bag, but I had to let that one go, as who knew what it was tied to and why he had it. I cut the bag of blow and allowed for some to sprinkle out, in the closet and up on the kitchen sink, cut into a few lines and then flushed the rest down the toilet. I then swept the room Elihu was in and scooped up his wallet and anything else that identified him, like his fucking French cigarettes. When I went back into the bedroom he was stirring on the floor so I tapped him hard with the butt of the P-5. I turned back to Clovis.

"I've never liked you, and now how ironic, as here we are. Do you have a decent sense of irony, Clovis? This wasn't in the script was it?" I got closer to him because I wanted to feel his fear, let it get into my speed-heated skin. "When Justin came to kill us he called Sylvia a nigger, a fucking tar baby," He winced at those words, " yea...can you imagine what she felt? The woman I was going to ask to marry me?" He was hyperventilating around the panties in his mouth now, eyes wide. Meredith actually sounded like she was praying.

"Sorry, cuz, no blindfolds or cigarettes. Just me"

I dragged Elihu up and walked-pushed him outside then sweeping his legs out to lay him down and made sure he wasn't going anywhere. I walked out to get the car dropping the wiped down piece with silencer in some bushes up the street, then completed what I felt was a perfect getaway. That silencer was really a fine little piece of engineering and I wondered what retired navy gunner's mate was making good side money cranking those babies out.

I had left the other two in the bathroom; Meredith in the tub and Clovis sitting on his prized toilet, which was his familiar place. I smiled at that bit of dark humor.

I had the information I asked for, but I didn't like it one bit. I had to pull over and throw up twice on the drive back.

Doc Krinberg

Chapter 52

I had a lot of swag from Clovis' little hidey-hole in the closet. I was actually counting it when my dad called with the terrible news about him and Meredith.

"Wow, that's terrible," I said.

He told me in a hushed tone because I was betting my mom was around that the cops found narcotics and a weapon at the scene. They found cocaine!! Executed gangland style!! To my dad this answered the question concerning Jack's business that Clovis, whom my father despised his entire life, was the real culprit in this drama. His parents were pretty much ex-communicated at this point by Jack and Nick's folks.

"Dad, I hear you. Just awful!" I supplied afterwards. I also added I wouldn't be available to take off work for the funerals but would send flowers. We said our goodbyes and I went back to counting.

It was a lot of money.

Doc Krinberg

Chapter 53

It was a cloudless day and hot. Argentina had beaten the Dutch in Buenos Aires 3-1, which meant I was on a roll. I had put some money down at the Asian-American Club with another bookie, some *katonk* guy, since François had passed. The drive across the Bay was leisurely and with no inversion I could see the top of the Golden Gate. The hills above Sausalito were brown and dry; drought conditions like the cocaine situation in the City and prices were going up.

I parked at the top of the driveway and walked down. The cypresses were still stooped and bent, the old guardians of the house like temple dogs in the still of this June day that 102 years ago saw George Armstrong Custer breath his last. I walked to the side gate and quietly entered. Issuing into the back I found four brilliant and mature Japanese Maples spaced across a back privacy fence. Underneath an elaborate pergola, an outdoor shower stood. The gate to the beach was open and the small path leading out was choked with holly and palmettos from years of neglect. I turned to the right, my attention on the rest of the yard and house and I didn't have to go very far.

She was sitting nude with the exception of a huge parasol hat that Lana Turner probably wore sunning herself on a yacht's bow. One hand held her cigarette in a long ebony holder and the other held either water with a slice of lime or a gin and tonic. I went with the latter. She looked up at me walking towards her. I stopped and stood over her, blocking the sun to give her eyes a break and offer her some shade.

"Are you going to kill me, Remy?" Her voice wasn't defiant but it certainly wasn't submissive. I reached out and handed her the letter I had taken from the mailbox, unopened.

"No Mrs. Bohannon, I'm here to make you a business proposition."

Chapter 54

The Ford panel van without windows looked like serial killer material but worked out beautifully. It resembled one of hundreds of contractor's vans roaming the city doing electrical or plumbing jobs. The aluminum ladder strapped to the roof was a nice touch. It also had a huge amount of square footage in the back for storage. The Weasel just had this knack for finding vehicles, I had to give him that. And now as I drove out 580 I found even the radio had good reception. I had one package in the back that I had to take east so I took my time. I found a classic rock station and just sang along respecting the speed limit, which every good citizen should do.

I hit 295 and that connected me to old 99 after doglegging down another old route. I stopped at a McDonald's drive thru in Manteca and then turned north. It was dark now in the east with that after glow still holding on in the west over the Pacific. The air was dry and hot and full of moths leaving smudges and splats over my windshield all the way to the Lodi city limits.

By the time I got to the park it was true night and driving to the designated rest area another car quickly flashed its lights on and off. I parked and reaching into the canvas workbag between the seats I took out the .38 hammerless, a small flashlight, the sheath of money inside its wrapping paper and a business card. I left the keys in the ignition and went into the back.

"Oh Lord, we're stuck in Lodi, again." I sang to the package.

He couldn't talk back because of the gag but I helped him sit up. I had the flashlight in between my teeth flooding his good eye and with my left hand I scattered the bills about the interior of the van. Then I put the flashlight under my chin monster light style, the way we'd do it when we were kids and scare each other at sleepovers. I was pretty sure I was scaring him.

Then I held up the card putting the light on it so he could see it clearly.

"I'm just going to leave this right here in your top pocket, Mr. Matranga, so the guys who find you will know where to go. Remember? You recommend these florists. Quick, efficient and always do great work, and they're down on the peninsula. Tell them no one sent you"

His eye was popping. "Dominic Rizzi sends his regards."

The .38 took a bit of his head with it and lodged into the frame and I dropped it so the cops could trace its history perhaps back to Justin. I went out the back doors and shut them. I took off my gloves and put them in my pockets, then went back and got the bag of garbage from McDonald's and took that too. The other car cruised up to me slowly.

"God, this is absolutely East Bumfuck. Who picked Lodi? Is this a bad joke?"

"Could you hear the gunshot?" She winced when I asked her that. Hanging out in the house hearing about criminal activity was one thing, being an accomplice was another.

"I heard a pop and saw the van rock a second, and had a horrible thought to that stupid saying, 'if this van's rockin'...'" That made me laugh.

"Everything copasetic city side?"

"We're fixed."

"Sweet."

After awhile, in the dark silence of the car, I started to be aware of her scent. It was sandalwood and so subtle it barely left her skin.

"I didn't think things would turn out the way they did. I had no idea how careless he was, and what happened. There was a Chinese wall between the two of us. He shuttered himself and kept me out."

"I know."

"Where does it go from here? Is this all over with?"

"Not sure. On his end there are reparations that need to be issued." I lit a cigarette and handed it to her, then lit my own. "What do you want in your future?"

"I want to be alive. I know its not going to be the same at all and Elihu and I were done, long time done. I just don't know why I didn't break it off before. Or did some of the things I did either."

"Security?"

"Yes, that. But familiarity too. Even at my age, or maybe more so at my age, there's fear of the unknown." She took a long drag. "Did you ever like me Remy?"

"You were always attached to Elihu, so I guess that just cancelled it out. Like we never dated friend's sisters in school. I was never fond of Elihu but as an associate I respected his relationship. I do like you, but I was also very wary too, to be honest."

"Yes, be honest. I know how I acted, but a lot of that was self-preservation, and Elihu wanted me to be a certain way. I found a perverse satisfaction in teasing you too. Sorry"

"I can see that."

"I'm scared of you, Remy. On the one hand I'm attracted to you, but seeing these things and knowing what you've done, capable of…I'm fearful. I thought you were my Pale Horse that day at Stinson. When you handed me my mail, I had this crazy vision of you waiting for me to read it, then killing me." She laughed. Then in a more sober voice, "Your girlfriend left you because of that night Justin came, didn't she? She saw behind the curtain."

My smile at her confession about impending doom vanished. "Yes, she did because of it. She saw something in me, behind that curtain as you say and it wasn't congruent with her world. I peeled the thin veneer off of my civilization." I pictured Mona in that parasol hat, "It was weird. I never thought I'd find you at the Stinson Beach house but when I saw you it seemed natural, I felt…" And she finished.

"At home?"

"Yes. I did." More than she realized.

"I'm forty-two, Remy."

"And?"

"I'm just putting that out there. You trusted me, even after all of this, and if I live thru this I think I have enough money to make a clean break. I'm not jumping from one swing to the next. If I'm independent, it means its voluntary. Yes?"

I threw my cigarette out the window, " Is there a chance Mr. Bohannon may reenter the picture?"

She sighed, "No. The younger Mr. Bohannon is in the Ia Drang Valley…forever." She said in a soft voice, "Let's let the dead stay dead, okay?"

"Wake me when we get to the Oakland Bay Bridge, okay?"

At Treasure Island, her hand found my head. I felt her fingers gently massaging me, pulling my hair back off my face. Opening my eyes the City, in its entire nighttime splendor lay before us.

"Remy, Welcome to the Boomtown."

Chapter 55

Elihu was a little busy after the Boys took him off to a safe place. There were a couple of things he had to do pronto. First, there was the issue of all the cash lost on the aborted trip, not so much the minimal needed for the trip and buy but the potential reward. Then there was the North Beach house. Corky decided he wanted the deed and didn't wish to do Matranga any favors, not liking him at their meet after I went to LA. and he had Elihu anyway, so that chip was off the table. The deed was signed over legally to Corky and he was sole owner now. Elihu had almost 2.5 million in a trust, not counting all his other assets like stocks, bonds, and real estate. I sat with Arthur and the Boys and had Mona declared a citizen, and out of bounds. It was agreed.

Elihu also sent $40k by wire to Marainos. There were only three things I wanted and Mona's whereabouts and safety being one, the money for Jack the second. I was surprised she was at the Stinson house, but she looked good with a tan and I was relieved that I didn't have to cap her. Spin had argued for clipping her because she gave him the creeps, but Corky just shook his head and countered half the fucking City gave him the creeps, honored my wishes and with a handshake much firmer than the one at the beach house we settled it. What I had planned at the Pan-American, they were all clueless about, and I let it stay that way. It didn't involve them.

If anyone was made for it, she was born to pull a honeypot scam. She had to return to the Pacific Heights house to grab some heels, a LBD and some makeup. She had told me she and Elihu had left in such a hurry when Justin's wife called screaming that he never returned from his 'quick city trip'. It meant one thing—he failed and Elihu expected me to show up on their doorstep any second like Sgt. Fury. Only Francois knew where he was.

The night before the major pick-up at the Pan-American, she was dressed to make a dead man crawl. The Weasel had tracked down Matranga to a nice little condo in the Marina District and it had been ass over tits to get this scam together at the last minute; the van, Mona, and the act.

The Weasel called me from a convenient pay phone to say Matranga hadn't returned as of yet—his parking stall still open and it was already 8 p.m. Fuck!! I had hoped that bastard would cruise home at a regular time but who in the hell knew with these guys. Mona was with the Weasel and so they waited. And waited.

At about 8:45 he pulled into his stall and Mona, popping out of the car went to work. Arthur told me later Matranga was a deer in the headlights.

" Excuse me? Oh my God, my car got a flat out here on the street, and luckily I pulled off safely but I need to be somewhere. Can you help?" Matranga, looking at her could barely stay in his skin, "Why not come up for a drink, I'll call a towing service and then I'll take you anywhere you want to go, Ms...?"

"Oh, I'm Marianne. Can you just take a look at it and, ohh my…that is a beautiful suit? Hugo Boss?" She cooed.

He preened a second, "Armani." Mona reached out her sinewy fingers, ran them up and down the lapel.

"A quick look, then upstairs?" She said breathlessly.

"Why not? Marianne…how's Ginger these days?" He chuckled.

Three minutes later he was face down on the back floor of the car, a head full of chloroform and zip ties around his wrists and ankles. As they drove, she asked Arthur in a low voice. "Did Remy kill François?"

"S-sort of."

"Will he kill Elihu?"

"I think the B-Boys have that answer." He answered truthfully. "And that d-depends on Elihu."

He said he could hear her whisper to herself, 'bye bye, Elihu.'

They took Matranga right up onto the Bridge and over to Stinson. When they were settled, I received a call. My turn now.

Doc Krinberg

Chapter 56

We had one guy on the graveyard shift. Shepard Little had been the night man for twenty-three years. During his shift they'd block off the up and down ramps with cars and place two across the entrance for security and the electric eyes on the ramps set off alarms if someone walked up or down. Some homeless people and thieves would attempt a breech and Shep would lock the office door and call 9-11. Other than that, he smoked cigarettes, listened to jazz and drank coffee. There were regular night owls and other late workers who would fall by and shoot the shit with him too.

I pulled in at 4 a.m. with the white van.

"Remy, what's up? You doin' some repair work, you moonlighting?" He asked after moving the cars for me.

I jumped out in coveralls, "Hey Shep." We shook hands. "I have to move some office supplies."

"Aight. I'll leave you alone."

So I emptied the safe into the van, locked it. I pulled a C-note off a roll in my pocket. I handed it to Shep. "If anyone asks who came in during the night, say me, the Italian boss and two Spanish speaking guys. Got that?"

"Se habla espanol, my man." We both laughed.

The morning guys came in, Shep cut out, and I appeared coming from Khalid's with a coffee. The guys asked about the van and I said it was a maintenance van for the Marine's Memorial Hotel, and I was going to move it later in the morning.

Polli rolled up at exactly 10, pissed off as usual; I came out of the office, smiled and waved.

"Hey, where were you this morning?" I asked yawning as he walked up. I didn't need to yawn as I was on that second black beauty.

He cocked his baldhead to one side, "The fuck you mean where was I? This is the time we planned on. Have you seen or heard from Matranga?" He was super agitated. On the street double-parked was a van with a giant arm out of the window, a hand like a skillet beating time to something.

"Yea, he called me in the middle of the night and said the time had changed and…" Then Polli was on me, and pushing me into the office. He pinned me against the wall, a forearm across the throat, a little pressure now, but I expected more in a minute.

"Now you fucking tell me, you Greek prick! NOW!"

"H-he-he called me like 3 a.m. and told me to get my ass down here. Said the time had been changed and he was in a hurry, didn't have the combo, cuz he has it written down, so I came here as fast as possible and he was here with two guys…" And here I described the SA cartel guys from Miami that Lorna had described to me. "…And we loaded the van. I asked where *you* were and he said to mind my own fucking business. That's it, Mr. Polli." He pushed off me with his forearm.

He screamed, "FUCK!" Pretty damn loud. He threw me out of the office while he made some calls. I hung out with the crew, chilling them out and springing for coffee.

"Who'll fly if I buy?" And Collier went next door to Khalid's. Polli came out of the office, stroking his mustache in thought.

"What kind of vehicle is it?"

"Big grey work van with a contractors name on the side on those big magnets? The ones that go on the doors."

"Name on it?"

"I think it was Widney or Wittney Bros, San Mateo." He took a deep breath.

"Has he done shit like this before? Called you, middle of the night stuff…open the safe?"

"A couple of times, yea. Onetime with those guys from last night, and once when he was with some women. He'd make me do it, said he needed money." I asked in a small voice, "Am I in trouble Mr. Polli?"

"Not yet. Listen, if Matranga calls or gets in touch with you, you call me. Immediately. Got that?" He wrote down his number on a Castle Street card like Matranga had given me.

"Will do!" I said enthusiastically. Then walking back out he banged the side of the white van in anger.

"What the hell was that about, Remy?"

I shrugged, "Beats me. These guys in corporate can barely keep their acts together." I went into the office and called the Weasel.

"All quiet on the western front." I drove the van back to Stinson; we unloaded the money, and later loaded up Matranga.

Chapter 57

The phone was ringing, and Polli picked it up sounding like he had ran to it.

"Hello? Who is this?"

A voice with a South American accent laughed into his ear after telling him what a stupid bastard Matranga *was* and how he deserved what he got.

"Your amigo has attempted his last rip off, and now the tables were turned." Polli was upset and frustrated.

"Vincent? Vince…is this you? Listen…we can make this better, no matter what's happened. Don't hold Phil's stupidity against us. We've been working a long time on this, Vincent. We're talking a *lot* of money!!" He started sounding frantic.

Then 'Vincent' started laughing again and told Polli where he could find his good buddy, hah ha ha…then called Polli an old bald whore, and a few more words in Spanish. Then Polli just snapped and started screaming. 'Vincent' finally hung up.

I was hanging outside the phone booth on the edge of the parking lot listening into this wild call. Berberian was just tearing up the card I gave him with Polli's number.

"Damn, I am impressed as an ex-marine at how salty old Polli got. You sounded pretty good. I guess living down south has its benefits. What was that you said in Spanish at the end?"

"*Si, senor.* Oh that? It's the end of a Steely Dan song, 'Only a Fool Would Say That.' Whoever V-vincent is, I guess he's in a world of shit now."

I shrugged. "Fuck em. Fuck em all."

"Back to S-Stinson this weekend?"

"Yep. I have to keep showing up for work or like a four day old fish, something will stink. Where's Mona?"

"P-p-pool."

I walked out the pool area and there she was, on her stomach, her Sartre paperback opened sitting spine up on the patio cement in front of her. Her head was cradled in her arms. In the time she and Elihu fled Pacific Heights until now I could see her hair had grown a little and the hint of grey in her roots showed. I'm not sure why but I felt more protective of her after seeing that.

"Hello Mona," I said softly. Her arms went out slowly and she stretched. She looked like a long, svelte cat. Sleepily she turned her head up, and sheltered her eyes but again I was standing in between her and the sun.

"Again you save me, as I lay here in your lee."

"Some things need saving. Other things we can't protect or hold onto if our lives depended on it."

"I'm sorry she's gone, Remy. She must've been something as you were pretty hardcore in the fidelity department. *Vous étiez un homme de poids parmi beaucoup de ceux qui flottaient juste sur le vent.*" She smiled.

"You do speak French. Which means?"

"You're a good guy."

"Are you still scared of me?"

"Silly me, being attracted to things that do scare me." I frowned.

"What?" She asked.

"I only wanted to protect her, to save us." I had one of those stupid what-if smiles.

"That old saying about the tiger and its stripes?"

"I've been brutally honest in your eyes. You've seen it. No Chinese wall."

"I'm getting used to that. You."

I looked down at her again. "I bet your hair would look beautiful if you let it go natural." I went back to the suite.

We stayed there at the hotel until the Thursday night, and then rolled back to Marin. I had a visit from Polli at the garage Thursday afternoon. It wasn't pretty. On Wednesday the cops in Lodi had found the van, Matranga and the tiny bit of loose cash and in a secret pocket of his suit, a vial of pure coke we missed. It was deemed a 'murder with ties to organized crime in California.' One reporter thought the Mexican Mafia was involved. There was no mention of the dropped piece I took from Justin. The cops would be working that one very quietly. It was an interesting fairy tale to read.

When Polli came in he brought with him an old, dapper safecracker from the 1940's who knew Mosler safes. None of us knew how to reset the combo, but this old geezer did and admired the safe as well. So now I was locked out of the safe, I was waiting to feel the whisper of the axe.

I sheepishly asked Polli if he wanted me to stay as manager and he blew up on me; threats, physical violence, etc. I just looked concerned as he went thru his list of reasons to fire me, kill me and fuck me. I told him I was union and he couldn't fire me. The older guy who reset the lock waiting in the backseat got out. He told Polli to 'get inna cahr.' And watched him storm back and get in slamming the door.

"Remy, right?" He had tired eyes, like marbles floating in oil with heavy lids.

"Yes, sir?"

"Dom, rest his soul, liked you. Said you were a good kid, good war record, could be trusted. You were a good soldier and did what your boss asked. Not your fault your boss sold you out, but you didn't know. Can I trust you, Remy?"

I got a little cautious here, "Yes, sir."

"I don't think the union would mind if you decided to seek employment elsewhere, capiche?" He smiled. "I don't think you and my son will get a long." He motioned towards Polli. "Recommend anyone?"

"Calloway is deserving."

He looked at me a little too long. "Sir?"

"You know, you could be Italian." And he walked back to the car.

And with that, I was done at the Pan-American.

Chapter 58

We counted the money that weekend and then I dropped by Corky's with Arthur, as we were almost neighbors from Stinson to Mill Valley.

"So?" I asked him.

"All is in order. We had a lawyer—actually one of the guys you met, and scared the shit out of by the way, help us out with the real estate fuck story. Everything was in his name as mommy and daddy number 34 are in LaLaLand up in Healdsburg and pretty clueless about the family fortune. So, after a few arguments from his lawyer, in which Elihu pulled an override, it's jake now. He took the occasion to make out a new will too." He smiled at his last remark.

"So when's the p-p-party?"

Corky laughed, "Every days a fucking party, Arthur, and when in hell are you going back south to look after my wife's interests? She's bitching because she needs more inventory." He turned to me, "Fuck, stay single Remy!"

He handed me a manila envelope about an inch thick.

"Paper works all there you just need to make with some signatures and get a notary to bless it, then you're in style. And I would make sure the inspection is good. Nineteen forty-six was a while ago." He went over to a peg on the kitchen wall. "Here, the pink slips in the dash signed. You just have to do the DMV shuffle." He handed me the keys to the Mustang. I looked at him.

"Finder's fee. You're Underdog, man...you saved the day. And I know you like it."

I smiled. "Much thanks."

"Stop by once in awhile, we'll sink a few or plot mass criminal activity."

As he walked me out, Arthur Berberian stopped me.

"That's a lot of money, Remy."

"Your share, or all of it?"

"Mine."

"You earned it. Start your own business and be independent."

"When are you flying south?"

"Day after tomorrow. Right now I really need to decompress." I put my hand out and he took it.

"*Vaya con dios*, Remy."

"*Vaya con dios*...Vincent."

He smiled.

Chapter 59

I had stashed the money in a storage place in South San Francisco because I still had a ton of Clovis' swag that I used as my WAM, my walking around money. I booked a flight to Panama and didn't look forward to it at all. I eventually ended up amending my ticket and spending a couple of days in Los Angeles. I took my, Jack and Nico's parents to Xavier Cugat's on the Row. They actually had a good time, and what the fuck, it was Clovis' money.

Flying south, my first port of call was Senor Marainos.

"Ahhh *Senor* Karras, I am so glad to see you again and to personally give you good news." The more I watched and listened to him the more I was convinced he was channeling Pedro Amendariz, Jr. in 'From Russia with Love.'

He explained how the jolt of 40k had pretty much cleared any logjam of judicial flotsam and jetsam and that Jack was tracking for an early September release. He just needed to hold on. I gave Marainos a nice even smile, asked if there was anything else he needed and after lying to each other for another few minutes, was informed my visit to the Waco had been set up. We said, 'Go with God,' didn't mean it and shook hands.

I'd brought down a suitcase full of books, magazines, candy and gum, cigarettes and hidden porn. I had extra cartons loaded with $50 bills for the guards as I was walking it thru, not Marainos.

Jack looked damn awful. I could see his arms had small dime sized discolorations from infected insect bites he'd scratched, and his hair had started falling out in some places. His eyes were bagged and while he was sporting a tan from hanging outdoors, he still looked unhealthy. He smelled like a mushroom cellar.

"This is fucking box office!" He exclaimed when he went thru the box like it was Christmas day. "A veritable cornucopia of goodies. Thanks Remy."

I nodded. He looked over at the guard. "Is that insane about Clovis and Meredith? My dad told me in a letter. What the fuck? Someone with a grudge, I mean it isn't like Clovis would win any personality contests?"

I just looked at him. The cat had gotten my tongue.

"So I'm outta here in September. Damn! Let's look to party that week! Fortune smiles on the Rat."

"Yea, fortune. Hey, let's drop all the window dressing, okay? Elihu's dead too."

He didn't look too good, "Wha'...?"

"Suicide, or assisted suicide. He had upset a lot of people and had become a liability. Like Nick."

His demeanor dropped from the pondering of Elihu's demise to my throwing Nick out there was a pressure drop, in his eyes and the room.

"Clovis told me Jack, and he had nothing but the truth left in his mouth when last he spoke. It was *you* who panicked over Nick's discussion with that DEA drip. *You* put the dogs on him. No one would've known outside you and Marainos, and that's not his job, to sort out the dramas surrounding a bust." His face looked as if his skin was burning and peeling off. "I know all of it. Those three; Elihu, Francois and Clovis burned you and everybody else for a pet project that went south. And all three are dead." He seemed to understand it finally. He started to speak but

I held my hand up.

"They dropped you and the jackal sent by the D-Boys just to keep an eye out and keep things smooth, because those three also set up the Weasel who once he was taken off the board, couldn't protect you anymore...this fucking jackal Justin went too far. You wanted Nick scared, but maybe the message got lost in translation or Nick just appealed to this fucking sadist. They sent him after Sylvia and me, too. You wanted him scared because you couldn't convince him when you saw him and he only wanted to help his big brother. Half the people you were protecting fucked you where you breathe. And now you're going to be here for what, another two months? You can think about it the whole time. And think about your parents too because they're broke down. Clovis is at Forest lawn if you want to mark his grave. No one in England wanted to claim Meredith, so she's there too."

He'd started crying. A couple of large drops hit the counter and he looked up blinking, failing to stem the tears.

"I think about it daily, every fucking minute.'

"I'm glad. That's a good thing. Oh, by the way, part of Elihu's legacy is bailing you out. He was real generous at the end." I stood up. "Okay, I'm done. You're set up monetarily; flat and bank account. All the money I quick grabbed out of there's back in your safe deposit. You're set."

He looked at me, the tears cutting clean furrows in his face against the embedded dirt.

"Let's just say goodbye here."

We looked at each other a few moments, and then I turned and left.

Doc Krinberg

Chapter 60

Even though it was almost Christmas, I still went out into the yard and sat in the chair in front of the rock garden; my favorite place. I hired a guy to come out to do some well-needed yard and arbor work. The hardscape was weeded and parts of the privacy fence repaired and replaced. I also had the wood on the front door revitalized and re-stained. I left everything at my Hugo Street flat with the exception of clothes, books, cassettes, LPs and my copy of the Gauguin's.

I still didn't have a TV.

In late November I read about Moscone and Milk being assassinated and down at the coffee shop on PCH the whole place buzzed about it. The papers couldn't let it go, and it was pushing Jonestown out of the news. This was fresh and it was across the Bay. When they published the list of who perished in Guyana, I burnt that copy of the Chronicle in a shit can in the backyard.

Mona let her hair start to go natural and she doesn't look the same. Her existence with Elihu had certain expectations that I don't have. It's unsaid but she's more relaxed now, enjoys the beach and rock garden, and even borrowing some of my shirts. I'm betting she used to wear Mr. Bohannon's shirts too. We maintained separate bedrooms but after Jonestown, I went to her room and without speaking she lifted her covers for me. I just lay down.

Doc Krinberg

About the Author

Gary "Doc" Krinberg was raised in California where he had a significant amount of dead end jobs to include hot pretzel salesman, strip club barker, parking lot valet, garage attendant and junkyard truck driver before embarking on a career in the US Navy as a hardhat diver that afforded him significant travel and exposure to many different cultures.Post navy, he pursued graduate and terminal degrees while teaching in various institutions in Japan, Hawaii and mainland America while helping to raise three sons and currently resides in Alexandria, Virginia, where he works at educational consulting, writing and editing poetry, enthused by the reemergence of the Oakland Raiders as a power in the AFC West. Doc is published in other Savant poetry anthologies to include Lost Tower, UK. as well as two novels with Aignos Publishing.

Doc Krinberg

If you enjoyed *The Winter Spider,* consider these other fine books from Aignos Publishing, an imprint of Savant Books and Publications:

The Dark Side of Sunshine by Paul Guzzo
Happy that it's Not True by Carlos Aleman
Cazadores de Libros Perdidos by German William Cabasssa Barber [Spanish]
The Desert and the City by Derek Bickerton
The Overnight Family Man by Paul Guzzo
There is No Cholera in Zimbabwe by Zachary M. Oliver
John Doe by Buz Sawyers
The Piano Tuner's Wife by Jean Yamasaki Toyama
Nuno by Carlos Aleman
*An Aura of Greatness: Reflections on Governor John A. Burn*s by Brendan P. Burns
Polonio Pass by Doc Krinberg
Iwana by Alvaro Leiva
University and King by Jeffrey Ryan Long
The Surreal Adventures of Dr. Mingus by Jesus Richard Felix Rodriguez
Letters by Buz Sawyers
In the Heart of the Country by Derek Bickerton
El Camino De Regreso by Maricruz Acuna [Spanish]
Diego in Two Places by Carlos Aleman
Prepositions by Jean Yamasaki Toyama
Deep Slumber of Dogs by Doc Krinberg
Saddam's Parrot by Jim Currie
Beneath Them by Natalie Roers
Chang the Magic Cat by A. G. Hayes
Illegal by E. M. Duesel
Island Wildlife: Exiles, Expats and Exotic Others by Robert Friedman

Coming Soon:
The Princess in My Mind by J. G. Matheny

www.aignospublishing.com

The Winter Spider

as well as these other fine books from Savant Books and Publications:

Essay, Essay, Essay by Yasuo Kobachi
Aloha from Coffee Island by Walter Miyanari
Footprints, Smiles and Little White Lies by Daniel S. Janik
The Illustrated Middle Earth by Daniel S. Janik
Last and Final Harvest by Daniel S. Janik
A Whale's Tale by Daniel S. Janik
Tropic of California by R. Page Kaufman
Tropic of California (the companion music CD) by R. Page Kaufman
The Village Curtain by Tony Tame
Dare to Love in Oz by William Maltese
The Interzone by Tatsuyuki Kobayashi
Today I Am a Man by Larry Rodness
The Bahrain Conspiracy by Bentley Gates
Called Home by Gloria Schumann
Kanaka Blues by Mike Farris
First Breath edited by Z. M. Oliver
Poor Rich by Jean Blasiar
The Jumper Chronicles by W. C. Peever
William Maltese's Flicker by William Maltese
My Unborn Child by Orest Stocco
Last Song of the Whales by Four Arrows
Perilous Panacea by Ronald Klueh
Falling but Fulfilled by Zachary M. Oliver
Mythical Voyage by Robin Ymer
Hello, Norma Jean by Sue Dolleris
Richer by Jean Blasiar
Manifest Intent by Mike Farris
Charlie No Face by David B. Seaburn
Number One Bestseller by Brian Morley
My Two Wives and Three Husbands by S. Stanley Gordon
In Dire Straits by Jim Currie
Wretched Land by Mila Komarnisky
Chan Kim by Ilan Herman
Who's Killing All the Lawyers? by A. G. Hayes
Ammon's Horn by G. Amati
Wavelengths edited by Zachary M. Oliver
Almost Paradise by Laurie Hanan
Communion by Jean Blasiar and Jonathan Marcantoni
The Oil Man by Leon Puissegur
Random Views of Asia from the Mid-Pacific by William E. Sharp
The Isla Vista Crucible by Reilly Ridgell
Blood Money by Scott Mastro
In the Himalayan Nights by Anoop Chandola
On My Behalf by Helen Doan
Traveler's Rest by Jonathan Marcantoni
Keys in the River by Tendai Mwanaka
Chimney Bluffs by David B. Seaburn
The Loons by Sue Dolleris
Light Surfer by David Allan Williams
The Judas List by A. G. Hayes

Doc Krinberg

Path of the Templar—Book 2 of The Jumper Chronicles by W. C. Peever
The Desperate Cycle by Tony Tame
Shutterbug by Buz Sawyer
Blessed are the Peacekeepers by Tom Donnelly and Mike Munger
Bellwether Messages edited by D. S. Janik
The Turtle Dances by Daniel S. Janik
The Lazarus Conspiracies by Richard Rose
Purple Haze by George B. Hudson
Imminent Danger by A. G. Hayes
Lullaby Moon (CD) by Malia Elliott of Leon & Malia
Volutions edited by Suzanne Langford
In the Eyes of the Son by Hans Brinckmann
The Hanging of Dr. Hanson by Bentley Gates
Flight of Destiny by Francis Powell
Elaine of Corbenic by Tima Z. Newman
Ballerina Birdies by Marina Yamamoto
More More Time by David B. Seabird
Crazy Like Me by Erin Lee
Cleopatra Unconquered by Helen R. Davis
Valedictory by Daniel Scott
The Chemical Factor by A. G. Hayes
Quantum Death by A. G. Hayes
Running from the Pack edited by Helen R. Davis
Big Heaven by Charlotte Hebert
Captain Riddle's Treasure by GV Rama Rao
All Things Await by Seth Clabough
Tsunami Libido by Cate Burns
Finding Kate by A. G. Hayes
The Adventures of Purple Head, Buddha Monkey and... by Erik Bracht
In the Shadows of My Mind by Andrew Massie
The Gumshoe by Richard Rose
Cereus by Z. Roux
Shadow and Light edited by Helen R. Davis
The Solar Triangle by A. G. Hayes
A Real Daughter by Lynne McKelvey
StoryTeller by Nicholas Bylotas
Bo Henry at Three Forks by Daniel D. Bradford

Coming Soon:
Cleopatra Victorious by Helen R. Davis

http://www.savantbooksandpublications.com

Made in the USA
Lexington, KY
02 May 2018